# *COVER*

I0647139

(Series Book 1) - The Truth Behind The Canvas: Four Women Unveil Their Truths About Suicide, Abuse, Infidelity, Pain and Victory.

Linda Diaz, Norra Prescott, Wendashia Ray, Tamara Stallings

Edited by Linda Cashdan

Copy Edited by Bethany Penn

Cover Design by Fabiola Jean-Louis

Cover Font Design and Layout by Gael Jean-Louis

V4 Global Enterprises

V4 Global Enterprises, LLC
Camp Springs, Maryland
v4gellc@gmail.com

## Dedication

This book is dedicated to God, our heavenly and earthly angels, and those who strive every day to live their best **vida** (life), preserve their **virtue**, realize their **value**, and embrace their **victory**.

I will lift up mine eyes unto the hills, from whence cometh my help.
My help cometh from the LORD, which made heaven and earth.
He will not suffer thy foot to be moved: he that keepeth thee will not slumber.
Behold, he that keepeth Israel shall neither slumber nor sleep.
The LORD is thy keeper: the LORD is thy shade upon thy right hand.
The sun shall not smite thee by day, nor the moon by night.
The LORD shall preserve thee from all evil: he shall preserve thy soul.

(Psalm 121: 1-7, King James Version)

# Prologue

For some time now—I think since I was a child—I have been possessed of the desire to put down the stuff of my life. This is a commonplace impulse, apparently, among persons of massive self-interest; sooner or later we all do it. And I am quite certain, there is only one internal quarrel; how much of the truth to tell? How much, how much, how much! It is brutal, in sober uncompromising moments, to reflect on the comedy of concern we all enact when it comes to our precious images! –Lorraine Hansberry

What does it take to finally make you break? To finally decide to let what exists in your mind but you hide in your life escape into plain site. So when others look at you they see the stories that serve as the building blocks that made you who you are. The things that make you feel like "God you made me, and then left me alone to deal with these brutal life lessons and heartaches to hide."

There is a common red thread composed of the forbidden truths that we hide to protect the beautiful image of ourselves that we have created for the world.

We are in the third hour of our book club meeting. There are seven empty bottles of wine, tears and we are still on the first discussion question.
 As one of us is going on to tell us for the 100$^{th}$ time how she makes six figures; I try to open the next bottle of wine (I promised myself that if she said the words "six figures" one more time I was going to sink into the next bottle of wine)… I try to keep my promises.
 Mrs. "all is perfect and white picket fences" is digging into her purse for her emergency wine opener.
 The one who needs the wine the most, won't even take a damn sip, she just smiles. I want to scream at her and say "just lose your fucking mind, you have the right to!" but she would rather fight the tears while she helps others try to avoid sharing her nightmare.
 I close my eyes and I wish I would have never been me, never made the decisions I made, tried so hard to hold on and embrace pain as my reality.
 Then the words came out like a flame "We have a story to tell" lets write our way through this hell.

Here we are with our pens, our post it notes, and a prayer.

# VIDA
## The Silent Killer-By Linda Diaz

When you see me, you see my smile and not the pain that has accompanied me through life, "The Real Cinderella Story".

Can you believe one of the happiest times in my life was when I was living in a foster home? Actually, it was our second foster home - the Smith Family, which my brothers and I were placed into, as the Department of Children Services did not want to split us up. Mother claimed her boyfriend (at that time) was beating us, so we were surrendered into Child Protective Services. Mrs. Smith taught me so much in the years I lived with her. She worked the midnight shift, full time, in a nursing home so that she could care for her kids and foster kids during the day. We attended school during the week and on Saturdays I went to work with Mrs. Smith to clean houses and deliver her Avon orders. *(Now I know where I get my cleanliness from.)* I also assisted with feeding the hogs, geese and chickens. On Sundays we went to bible school and church.

I remember, as clear as glass, the day I was removed from her care and made to go live with my biological mother. I cried and cried and begged them not to take me away, but I had to go. Mrs. Smith gave me a hug, told me she loved me and said, "Remember; always treat others the way you want to be treated".

It sounds crazy, but, yes, I was taken out of my foster home, kicking and screaming because I did NOT want to leave. I knew exactly where I was going, back to a place I was not wanted. Child Protective Services had been told so many lies, but the person they did not listen to was me. There are many horror stories about being raised in the Foster Care System, but mine was a good one. While living in Foster Care, I was not left alone, ignored, beaten; nor was I left to be molested by mother's boyfriends. So, it's not like I was going back to live a magnificent life with my loving mother. To be honest, it was Mother's new boyfriend who insisted that a daughter belonged with her mother. They left my brothers in Foster Care.

Soon after I was returned to my mother, along came the birth of her and her boyfriend's first child. Along with cleaning the house, shopping for groceries and washing and folding the clothes, child care was added to my list of chores. At the age of 11, I took the baby to the sitter each day and walked to school. On the way home from school, I would pick up the baby and care for her until Mother returned from work. During her weekend visits, I was also given the responsibility of caring for my young step sister, whom I came to adore. It was so nice having little sisters and taking care of them was my favorite chore. There were no disposable diapers, only the cloth diapers with safety pins. There was nothing like being able to hold the baby, feed her and give her baths. If there was anything good that came out of living with Mother, it was being able to care for my baby sister and my little step sister. I made sure to care for them and to protect them. Being a big sister was such a gift and I wanted to be the best big sister.

We always had a dog; Doberman pinschers to be exact and I loved walking the dogs. It was so much fun to me; running and having them chase me around. When I was young, I never realized how smart dogs were and it was great that I could win when I ran with them. The dogs loved chasing me, it was awesome, and when I jumped the fences they could not make it. That is when I realized, as they grew, bigger and stronger, so did their intellects. Eventually the times I jumped the fence and turned back and laughed at the dogs, stopped. Why? Well, let's just say that the Dobies not only became wise to my trick, but became absolutely athletic. The last time I jumped the fence to turn and laugh at them, I was being pounced on, as they jumped the fence and laughed at me. I loved taking care of the dogs, as all they ever showed me, was love.

There were times, if I was tired, didn't move fast enough or answer quickly mother felt the need to take out all her anger out on me. I often wondered, as a former foster child, why Child Protective Services did not have follow up visits, when placing a child back into an abusive environment. I would answer the phone, hoping it was my case worker, but it was never was. I felt all alone. There was no one to call or speak too after one of Mother's fits of rage. "Why me?" I would ask God. "Why am I here except to be mother's personal punching bag? Where is my father? Why doesn't he come save me from this life I am living?"

All I wanted was to be held and loved. I dared not ask about my father, as that would be another fit of rage to answer to. Everything was my fault. Mother's boyfriend did not drink or smoke. He told her to stop drinking and smoking, so she did. As many smokers know, it's hard to stop such bad habits, and I was the only one the rage could be taken out on.

After a while, there were many arguments and fights, so the time came when Mother's boyfriend, insisted that she stay home and care for their child, as she was then pregnant with their second child. There was a short placement of another stepsister with us, who was awesome and made me feel safe. This step sister was great to me and accepted me as her sister. I began to think, maybe things wouldn't be too bad with my step sister living with us, but that soon changed as Mother's boyfriend sent her back to live with her own mother.

This life began to take its toll, and I felt the darkness taking over me, so I ran away. I went to the home of my younger brother's father. Of course, Mother found me, beat me in the middle of the street, almost choked me to death and threatened to kill me, if I ever tried to run away again. That was when I accepted that I had no choice but accept Mother's terms, because no one was going to help me. I not only accepted my beatings, but after time, I began to think I deserved them.

In school, I wore clothes that did not show the bruises, and I stayed to myself. I was not allowed to have friends nor have anyone come to my house. In time, I was allowed to have one friend. I didn't realize it was because her father was a dentist. I was allowed to spend the night at her house, but I was told never to speak of our family business to anyone, that what went on in our home was our business and no one else's. This friend and her parents were very kind to me. I dared not tell them the bad things that happened to me in order to keep the friendship. I learned to live in silence. It wasn't until years later I learned Mother went to my friend's dad for dentistry work.

A step brother, who ran away from his mother, came to live with us. I was never treated like a daughter. I never knew who was coming until the person arrived. I'm pretty sure that since my step brother was there, Mother must have insisted that my older brother be allowed to come too. My younger brother remained in Foster Care. So I was finally reunited with one of my brothers, whom I had missed terribly since our separation from the Smith home. I was thrilled that maybe things would be different now that I had my own brother back. *Boy, was I wrong!* Nothing changed except I was beaten more! My step brother and my brother were free to come and go as they pleased, but I remained with all the household chores and tasked to care for Mother's children. The boys often played cruel games and did things in the house because they knew Mother would always believe them, when they blamed me. The truth did not matter to her, especially when it was two against one.

The darkness insisted on living within me, so we roomed together in silence. Living in this home was a daily horror; who would want to keep doing it? I prayed every night for God to take me away but there was never an answer. It became apparent that I was of no importance to this family and I was always treated as the outsider, but yet I felt a need to be accepted. I did whatever I could to keep them happy. I was only permitted to spend the night in a few people's homes.

As time passed, I learned to cope with my life and do whatever I could to spend time away from them. In other words, I became a great actress! I was provided with rules and was told never to say that we were a blended family and to keep my mouth shut. I would travel with the family and take care of Mother's children, like a personal nanny. If I wanted to go anywhere, it had to be with my step brother and my brother. As long as I stuck to the rules and did not do things to enrage Mother, I was okay. I was never to speak to any adult who visited our home and to stay out of sight. I never understood why, but I learned to adapt to the rules, and that is how I was able to spend time with other families. As long as I never mentioned what happened to me, when home, I was able to spend some nights away. It was only during my short stays with other families that I noticed the light taking away my darkness. As part of a blended family and Puerto Rican, I was not really accepted and only a few showed me kindness.

I treasured my stepfather's mother. She was an angel and never saw me as anything but another grandchild. I looked forward to being with her and a few of my cousins who were great to me and considered me just another cousin. I carry them in my heart for all time. There were others on that side of the family who looked like they hated me, so I never really bothered with them. On my stepfather's side I also had a couple of aunts and uncles who were great to me and accepted me. Although I did not speak of the things that caused my darkness, I felt the light shine through when I was with others, as if an angel reached down to me and was telling me, "Just hold on!"

We moved again, and my mother and stepfather had their third child. This was the golden child, deemed to be their perfect child, with beautiful hair and a light complexion. This was the one who looked most Spanish, my youngest sister. As the population of the area where we moved was all black, things became worse for me. I was placed in an all black school, not that it mattered to me, but that didn't last long. I was asked to leave the school and told I needed to be placed in a school with more children who looked more like me. I later found out that because I was Spanish and got a lot of attention from boys, it was causing a disturbance in the school. Considering my mother's boyfriend was black and my foster families were black, I felt at home! I didn't feel I got a lot of attention, especially since one of the rules was that I was never to have a boyfriend! The first time I was caught speaking with a boy was on the phone. Mother's boyfriend slapped me and hung up the phone. Little did he realize I was only calling for that day's class work because I had been absent from school to take care of his daughter. I was humiliated for the rest of that year; I could never even look up at the boy again, and he seemed to feel the same way. I don't know who was more embarrassed, he or I?

As I got a little older, I learned to be quiet and not say much or fight when it came to others. I learned not to make a fuss or complain. Since my opinion never mattered, I learned to just do what I was told. I went back to my previous High School and I began the two hour bus ride, one way, every day back and forth to school - a total of four hours a day traveling by Metro to and from school.

I did whatever chores were given to me - walking to the grocery store, cleaning, caring for the kids or doing the girls' hair for the next day. Doing my sisters' hair was also a chore because my mother did not know how to care for coarse hair. After all my chores were completed, I would stay up, until about midnight, to complete my studies and do my homework, and then have to start my day all over again and be on the 4:45AM bus to Fort Totten station and transfer buses to get to Beltsville. Sometimes, in order to delay my arrival, I would find other places to go to before heading back home.

One time, I met a boy, and I thought he really liked me, but it turned out he had a girlfriend. She and I did not fight but we got back at him a better way; by becoming friends! To this day, she has always been a constant in my life. Her mom was not there but her aunt and uncle loved her dearly. My mother hated this friend and she never cared for my mother. The closer we got, the more ashamed I was of all that my family did, so I would drift in and out of her life. I truly believe she was a gift of light, like the footprints in the sand, because every few years we would run into each other and become close again.

I was 16 years old when my senior year began in high school and it was I all I could do to hold on a little bit longer. I was not perfect. Sometimes I stopped and went to friends' homes for small visits before getting back on the bus to get home in time for chores. As time passed, I met a new friend, and she was kind too. She came from a good family and since they were Spanish, my mother and stepfather did not mind if I spent time with her.

I missed a lot of school to attend school events with my sisters and accompany them on their school trips. I did not mind too much, as long as they were safe, because I wanted to protect them. In the end, however, with all the moving and missing so much school, I had to attend regular school during the day and take night classes in order to graduate on time.

It was at that time that I met Hines, and he made all the darkness inside go away. Since I was never allowed to have a boyfriend, I kept Hines secret from everyone in my family, especially my brother and step brother. The last thing I needed was to be the focus of Mother's anger, again. Hines was 19 years old and he was training to be a professional boxer. One day he had the courage to come to my house to meet my mother's boyfriend, just to introduce himself, as one boxer to another. They had no idea that he was someone special to me. Hines was kind, loving and a gentleman. I was young and not interested in becoming sexually involved, and Hines respected that and would only give me a kiss when he saw me. He made all my pain go away, so you can imagine how I felt when I was suddenly not able to reach him. After many calls to his home, with no answer, I will never forget the day his mother answered and gave me the news that Hines had died from a brain aneurism.

My heart was crushed, and there was no one I could share this with because I was not allowed to have a boyfriend. I could not attend the funeral for Hines, nor send his mom and sister a card or give them a hug. I cried on the bus as I went to and from school. I suffered in silence in order to spare myself the wrath of Mother again. It took everything I had to keep going and hope that there was a reason to hold on to this meaningless life.

I lived in a house where I was the caretaker, nanny and fall person for all the wrongdoings from the sons. I found some joy in taking care of my little sisters, especially the middle one, but as time went on, each one changed and I watched as the boys picked favorites and played the girls against each other. After a while, I gave up on trying to teach the girls to stick together because no matter what lie the boys told, I was the one who received the wrath of Mother's hatred.

I did not dare ask about my own father because that always resulted in a beating. Mother stated I disrespected her husband by even asking about my father. "He is your father and no one else," she would yell. Along with the beating came all the reasons I was hated:

1. "You look like your father."
2. "You're ugly and no one will ever want you."
3. "I wish you were never born."
4. "I never wanted you, and if it weren't for your father I would have aborted you."

I wasn't invited to the ceremony, so I never knew when Mother and her boyfriend married, not that it really mattered, since I was told to call him "father" from the day I got home from foster care. I learned that lesson when I first moved back in with them, and a kid outside asked me if he was my father and I said "no". I was slapped in the face by her boyfriend, and when he told Mother what I said, I was beaten even more. To be honest, although never great, things were better when my stepfather was home. Mother hardly bothered me then and neither did the boys. I studied as much as possible did my chores and as long as I followed the rules, I knew I only had to hold on until I was 18 years old when I could leave.

Finally, final exams were done, and I was able to attend the prom. As a favor one of stepfather's friends had his little brother go to prom with me, and even hired a limo to take us to prom. Mother took me to JC Penny to get my prom dress and to the hairdresser to get my hair done. I had never been allowed to cut my hair, so when Mother left me at the salon, I told them to cut off all my hair. I felt I had already endured a lot. What could Mother do to me that she had not already done? I got in big trouble for cutting my hair. If not for the guy attending prom with me and the prearranged transportation going to the prom would have been cancelled.

I was so proud of myself for cutting my hair, and I found that graduating was a special triumph to me. I had not given up. Graduation day was fabulous. There were parties that I was invited to, but was not allowed to attend, but I really didn't care. I had gone through hell to graduate and I viewed it as a great personal achievement. Both my brothers were older, and neither had graduated.

It was the summer of 1986 and I was finally permitted to go to the movies with a friend, and to go out with her brother a few times. When I did, Mother said I had to marry him. I did not mind; I would have done anything to get out of their house.

He was a kind man and protective, and he had a daughter. I had just turned 18 years old and was a stepmother to a 5-year-old little girl. As I had spent many years helping to take care of Mother's children, that was an easy task. We lived in the basement in a house, and I had no clue what I was doing. I had pretty much grown up with no advice whatsoever about anything - how to work, how to care for myself, how to save money, let alone how to be a wife at 18.

I found out that my husband was also selling and using drugs and I am grateful that he was never abusive to me in any way. He was a good man. He did not cheat on me, and he deserved so much better than an inexperienced teenage girl, as a wife. I began to become confused. I had become used to being told what to do and accustomed to the abusive treatment of my family. No matter what I did, the darkness always returned, and it began consuming me. I felt alone and worthless, and I felt the need to rid myself of the pain that I had hidden inside for so long. I said a prayer, swallowed almost a whole bottle of Tylenol and off to sleep I went. The pain in my head and confusion of life had me spinning, and I just needed it all to stop. Taking several pills did not help, so I didn't think taking a lot of the pills would hurt any.

The next thing I remember was my husband placing me in the tub to help me feel better. I had no idea taking so many pills were harmful, as I just needed the pain to stop. It was at that time I realized that God had a plan for me; I just did not know what it was. It seems that I am great at running away from my problems, so, I decided to be all I could be and I joined the Army. As it happened, I passed a recruiting office and dropped in. I spoke with Sergeant Smith about enlisting, he had me take a pretest and I did well. After chatting more, he asked me to take the ASVAB and test to enlist and that is how my journey in the Military began. I did whatever I could to get away from everyone and everything that had clouded my mind and kept the darkness near. It was time to start being strong and understand that I had endured and overcome so much trauma, abuse, abandonment, and isolation I could not give up now.

The feeling was amazing. I felt so free, even though I did not realize exactly how much God loved me, even then. Not every family is great and we can't pick our families, for sure. I did not have the greatest teacher in life so I was winging how to live. Basic Training (BT) was the best time in my life, and I enjoyed the blood, sweat and no tears. I never missed anyone like I missed my little sisters and that has always caused a ripple in my life. I sent my sisters gifts so that they knew how much I missed and loved them. I also sent Mother a teddy bear, for she was pregnant again. I learned a lot in basic training - from survival tactics to discipline. After so many years of having Mother punching, screaming and cursing in my face, the drill sergeants were a piece of cake. Was I a great soldier? Hell, yes, I was! After hundreds of pushups, I finally learned to stop beginning my sentences with the word, "Yo"! The military was the best thing that ever happened to me, and I am grateful for everything I learned.

During the graduation ceremony, from basic training, there stood Mother. You couldn't miss her belly, as she was as huge as a house with another son. I really did not want to be around them or my husband but the military had invited them. I felt so bad being forced to marry him and I was completely unaware of exactly how much he loved me because my mind was so twisted and distorted from my upbringing. Love was something I had no true understanding of, when it came to a man. To be honest, my head would spin out of control because I had no clue how to truly love anyone but my little sisters.

Finally, graduation day was over and off to I went to Advance Individual Training to become a Heavy Wheel Vehicle Repairman. The one thing my step uncles loved to do was work on cars, so I longed to do the same. Little did I know that the military was still "A Man's World." I was one of three female mechanics in a company of about 500 men. That was both awesome and grueling at the same time. I felt as though I was back in basic training. I worked out harder and did more pushups, running and workouts than anyone else. After graduating from Advanced Individual Training, it was off to the 2nd Armor Division in Ft Hood, Texas. I was shuffled around between companies, but no matter, because I had to live off base. There weren't safe quarters for a female, as it was an all-male company.

I believe that was the most fun I've ever had. I was going out to nightclubs and yet making my 5 a.m. PT formations. At eighteen, I was very naïve about life and what I should or should not do. I made many mistakes. While partying and enjoying my life and doing some things I should not have done, I managed to have unprotected sex and got pregnant.

My pregnancy was a complete shock and by the time I realized it, I was far along. After multiple urine tests showing positive, it took the ultrasound and the heartbeat to make me realize the baby was real. I found out I was six months pregnant. Yes, crazy to hear but honestly, all I did was work, work out and dance all night long. I had the most amazing physique with about 2% body fat and abs you could wash clothes on. So, no, there was no showing that I was pregnant except maybe a larger bust size than normal.

Once I found I was pregnant the only thing I could do was think, wow, I need help. So, what did I do? I went back home, thinking my mother would help me to through this sensitive and confusing time. It was during this time, I ended up meeting a guy I thought was a good guy. He was friends with my brother. Even though I was pregnant, he still adored me and said he wanted to be there for me. I was initially given the due date of July 27th but the baby was not ready to come out. So I was given a date for inducing labor. On August 17, 1988, my beautiful little girl was born. She weighed 6lbs 13oz and was 22 ½ inches long. I know, right? Where in the world was she because my belly was not large at all, for a baby that long. I also became part of the DC Army National Guard at that time, and loved my company.

I tried living at home, but Mother made things so complicated. It's not like I was a lazy, good for nothing drinking and drug-using daughter. I was a brand new mother with a beautiful daughter. It took me a while to create a name, so I decided on Loryel Marie. She was an angel and the most beautiful baby. Of course, because my stepfather was OBSESSED with Whitney Houston, they demanded that I name my child Whitney. I stood my ground and was NOT naming my child a name I didn't like. Mother also had my baby brother, who was one year old, and I did not want to go home, as he had a virus that I wanted to keep Loryel away from. So, I went to a friend's home, but because Mother had this unspeakable way of getting to me, I ended up going back to Mother's home.

When Loryel was three days old, she caught the virus. Mother swore Loryel would not catch the virus because my baby brother was no longer contagious. I had no car, so mother dropped me off at Washington Hospital Center as my baby girl had a 106.0 degree fever. Loryel's fever was so high that the nurses placed her in bucket ice to stop the fever from climbing and her from possibly developing brain damage. As the fever was so high, the remaining umbilical cord fell off from Loryel's belly. The nurses now began the fight to find a vein to start an IV. I had to leave the room and go down the hall when they placed the IV in the soft spot of my newborns daughter's head. Nine long days later, Loryel got better.

Released from the hospital, I was mentally exhausted and traumatized from such an ordeal. I went back home. When I was sitting on the bed thinking of my 12-day-old baby girl and the amazing strength God gave us to get through this, I turned my head in time to see Mother's hand go past my face and smack Loryel. She did not mean to smack Loryel; she meant to slap me because I had not responded to her while she was speaking to me. I placed Loryel on the bed and jumped at Mother, ready to beat the hell out of her, but by this time, my stepfather made it into the basement to split us up. I immediately left mother's house and sought refuge with friends, bouncing around between friends' homes until I found a room to rent. At this time, I worked and took care of Loryel and continued to date the same guy I met, while I was pregnant... until I found out he was cheating on me. I ended things with him, or at least thought I had. He began to attack me when I was gathering my belongings, and I had to call my brother to come help me out of his apartment.

By this time Mother and I were on speaking terms again. One day Mother called and asked me to pick up one of my sisters and I decided to stop on the way back and let my sister get an ice from Seven Eleven. As I was waiting for her to get back in the car, my ex-boyfriend showed up. He was talking nicely to me, through the car door. I felt no threat at that time but I told him I had to leave to take my sister home, but I would come back to talk to him. He must have felt that I was just telling him that so that he would let me go, because he began to attack me, breaking through the driver's door window and punching me repeatedly in my head. I do not remember the actual incident. I believe God created a shield to keep that severe trauma from my memory. I only remember getting to Mother's home, waking up in an ambulance and being in the hospital. I do recall it took me months to recover from the concussion, hematomas and lacerations.

All he got was a year's probation for first degree assault. Did the DC Police Department care that my face was black and blue, swollen from a fracture, concussion and multiple lacerations? That was when my disbelief in the justice system began. I moved and stayed away from him and did what I needed to do to take care of me and my child.

Times were hard and as long as I was in the military I went through multiple caregivers for Loryel. I reached out to Mother, as she was a stay at home mom to help care for Loryel, but she refused to help me. I did what I had to, and at time often had to pay sitters/caregivers to keep Loryel overnight, as I had no car to get back and forth. One of my fellow soldiers was awesome and always offered to help me with transportation. My unit was great and all my fellow soldiers were pretty cool and they helped us tremendously.

I dated here and there but nothing too serious. I did meet one gentleman I thought was my knight in shining armor. He proposed, and soon after I asked to be transferred to Georgia, where his family was located. I also caught up with an old friend, who was also married and living in Georgia. It was great seeing my friend and being in Georgia. Then came the nightmare. I was arrested for theft as my by then ex-fiancé, turned out to be part of an auto theft ring. In the end he made sure I was cleared, but Loryel had to stay with my mother and stepfather for a little while until I was released and able to go back and get her. The charges were dropped against me and I picked up the pieces but I felt the Darkness was always trying its best to creep into my life. As I looked at my beautiful daughter, however, I was determined that the Darkness would never grab a hold of me. My step brother came to live with me, supposedly to help with the bills. Instead he helped my fiancé cheat on me and served as a cover for him. By this time, I had no choice but go inactive reserve from the military, and I began working with the Georgia Lottery.

My brother did not work, but he began buying a lot of computers and music equipment and he said he was working in the music talent business. I was gullible and believed my stepbrother cared, so I didn't make him pay his half of anything. One day he said he needed to go back to DC and that he would be back in a few days. I began getting the bills, and as a single mother, I could not manage the high phone, utility bills and the rent. I called him, at our parent's home, and he swore he would be back before the bills were due. Three weeks later, I began to panic, as the bills were all due and with rent, I was overwhelmed.

I phoned Mother's house, in DC, to ask when he would be back and he said he had no idea. We agreed that I could pawn his computers and equipment, in order to receive his half of the money owed. Suddenly, I got a knock on the door late at night to arrest me for grand theft. I was sick to my stomach as I had no support system and had to ask the sheriff if I could ask my neighbor to keep Loryel. My step brother had filed theft charges, against me, for stealing his computer equipment. I called Mother's home to find out they provided him the transportation back to GA to "do what he needed to do", as I was told.. I guess my going to jail must have been a laugh for them all. I demanded they pay my bail, which they did. In the meantime the investigation showed that my step brother lied and the charges were deferred after the pawn shop owner verified my story.

Back to work and each day was a struggle, but I felt I had to do right by my daughter and that is all I could think of. I stopped speaking to my family, again. I missed my sisters but I just could not allow the darkness back into my life. As the lottery grew, so did my hours, I did what I could to care for my baby girl. My family decided to visit and my youngest sister stayed with Loryel and me. That sister had fun with Loryel, and it was good to have someone to play with my daughter. When it was time for my sister to go back home, I thought it would be a good idea to send Loryel home with my sister. This way Loryel was not with strangers and she was with actually family. That did not last long. I missed my baby girl and after a couple of months, I brought Loryel back home with me. I placed Loryel in school and I qualified for before and after care for her to stay in school after school was out. I vowed never to leave her again as my life had no meaning without my daughter. As time passed, my little sisters and I stayed in touch, and I always missed them, terribly. At some point Mother suffered a mild heart attack or anxiety attack. My sisters cried and cried and begged me to moved back home, as they were scared about something happening to mother. So, I did. I resigned from the lottery, broke my lease, packed up my home and moved back to help Mother.

I enrolled Loryel in a DC school and helped mother run errands and did whatever she needed, so that she could rest. I got a job with an accountant and was able to work hours that allowed me to get off at 3p.m.

That did not last long. Living with Mother became a nightmare, again because she was taking her aggression out on me, and once again I let her. I moved into an apartment with a friend and we did well for a long time. We did a lot and we both took care of Loryel. I reached out to Loryel's dad and we did attempt to keep in touch as I always wanted Loryel to know her father. It was never a secret that he wasn't ready to be a father. We would always speak on the phone and I had never asked for anything but his time. However, after about six years I thought I would ask for some financial assistance, and, wanting to do this the right way, I went through the courts.

I really had no idea what I was doing. I went to this place to have blood work done for paternity. The courts sent me paperwork to do the blood work again, as the paternity tests did not match. I was so upset and confused that I decided to just shove this blood test into the trauma part of my shield and continue forward with being mom and dad.

A couple of years later, as my friend and I always traveled back and forth to New York City, I met a guy who I believed was good a guy. By this time, I was back on speaking terms with Mother and I introduced this man to the family. I knew he had been in prison and I thought he was honest with me. After losing his job in New York City, he called me and we discussed him changing his probation from New York to Maryland. We completed the transfer paperwork and Loryel really liked him, so I thought okay, we will be all right. My family loved Anthony. He and my brother became best friends.

My friend moved out in order to allow my brother to move in. So I was living with my daughter, my boyfriend and my brother. It was then, I met another friend and she had two daughters. We became friends because people often confused us as our names were similar. At one time, I was hated because others thought I was her. Erin and I also became good friends and I often watched her girls. I loved having her girls, as they were always a treasure and Loryel loved them too. My friend who moved out was not happy that I was friends with Erin so she and I began to drift apart. I did not mind that she moved out, because I was not a "go out and party person," and she was. I never stopped her from being friends with my brother or Anthony. They always hung out and I had no issue with that.

One night I woke up to find my car gone along with my brother and Anthony. I paged them with no answer. I stayed up and waited for them to get back home. When Anthony and my brother returned home, I was upset and asked where they had gone in my car? Out of nowhere, Anthony slapped me for arguing back with him, slapped me so hard that I lost my hearing. He immediately asked for forgiveness and said it would never happen again. He blamed it on drinking too much and said that my friend gave him some drugs, which caused him to lose control. I went to the doctors and was told I had a perforated ear drum and provided medicine and follow up care. Anthony promised to never touch me again and for a long time, Anthony kept his word. Little did I know he also kept something else—a secret relationship with another girlfriend.

I believe that is when the shame of allowing myself to be abused and hiding it began to allow some darkness back into my life. As I lived in shame, within myself, this caused my self esteem to decline. My family loved Anthony and he was good with Loryel, so I thought, one mistake was okay and I agreed to move on. I kept working and making sure Loryel was always taken care of.

I began to visit and allow her to spend time with the family. My middle sister was always the one I felt an immense bond with, a bond which could withstand any storm. Never allowing my sisters to know that I had been molested as a child, I began to allow Loryel to spend the night, but always whispered to my middle sister to please keep an extra eye on Loryel and that Loryel could only sleep with her. Off and on Mother always did things to upset me, and there would be times where I did not take Loryel to visit.

There were many times I asked Mother to stop telling people about my life and what I was going through, Mother told me to shut up and that she would say what she wanted. I tried not to place Loryel in the middle of the personal attacks that Mother was always making against me.

There came a time when my mother and stepfather placed a down payment on a condo, which they no longer wanted. They were going to lose their deposit, so they asked me if I wanted to purchase it. I applied, got the loan and soon owned my condo. When I saw my mother's friends, however, they all congratulated me on the condo my parents had bought for me. I was being told how lucky I was that my parents bought me a place to own! I never said anything because I just did not feel like dealing with Mother and her lies.

By this time, I had also told my brother that he needed to find a new place to live as I could not continue to take care of him. He had been with me for four years, making no financial contribution. He did adore Loryel and she adored him, but enough was enough. I also insisted that Anthony stopped being fired from so many jobs as we needed more money. I had been the only one working fulltime and basically taking care of four people on my salary. About a year after I bought the Condo, I found out I was a little over 3 months pregnant. So, as my brother finally moved into Mother's home in DC and I was preparing for a new baby, I saw the change in Anthony. He became angry. One day, after work, I was exhausted and as Anthony lay on the couch and watched TV, I asked for help around the house. He threw the remote control at my stomach and began screaming and yelling at me. I cannot explain the feeling of hatred and helplessness that overwhelmed me at that moment. I took Loryel and got in the car and went for a drive. I had no idea what to do and had no one to speak too as my family adored him and always took his side. When I returned home, I was honestly surprised as Anthony was not just apologetic but also asked me to marry him. At that moment I thought this was what I wanted, to be married and not bring another baby into this world as a single mom. So I put all the bad behind me, and agreed with Anthony to begin new and fresh, going forward.

For nine years, Loryel had wished for and prayed for a father and a sister, and after rubbing on a Buddha's belly, her dream came true. During a very difficult time, as I struggled to work and balance taking care of Loryel and me, my pregnancy was the calm in my stressful life. I spent the rest of pregnancy happy and with no problems. I was not angry with any family members and all was going well.

We married in 1997 and my stepfather insisted on having dinner at Red Lobster, after the wedding at the courthouse. I had a great job with a wonderful boss and the most loving team of co-workers. Life could not have been better for me as I thought: finally, we were going to be okay.

In December that year, Anthony got fired from his job, again, but swore he would get another job and not to worry. He said he was fired because he was caught using clients phones for calling back and forth to New York City, always checking up on his father. I felt bad for him and did not get upset. Soon afterwards he began working again as well as a part-time job with my brother.

On January 26, 1998 the new baby was eager to be with us. My labor went so quickly that I was asked to stop pushing, as my baby wanted to make her debut without the doctor. The doctor finally arrived and it was at that time that God blessed us with a beautiful and healthy baby girl and we named her Lauryn. I wanted to name her close to Anthony's mother name, Laura, who had passed away from cancer.

Around this time, Anthony's brother moved to Maryland from New York. He was a really good guy to me and the girls. After a little while, I noticed the tension between Anthony his brother. One day when he was out, his brother began filling in some blanks with regards to Anthony having girlfriends in New York City and that he was not as good a guy as he was pretending to be. I began asking about these things and it became heated. They got into a fight and Anthony stabbed his brother. This incident lead to Anthony being charged with assault against his brother.

I had taken the girls over to my parents and asked that they keep an eye on them as I attempted to assist Anthony. Upon returning to pick up the girls, I saw Mother was a bad mood and I was tired. I just wanted to pick up Loryel and go home, as they live 55 miles from my condo. Once again, Mother was yelling at me and walking towards me as if she was going to hit me, again, and this time I was a 30-year-old adult! As I stood on the front lawn, I warned her not to touch me and at that exact moment, she slapped me. I picked her up and slammed on her on the ground and proceeded to pounce on her. While everyone was pulling me off of Mother, the witch was pulling my hair. We got in the car and proceeded home, where a sheriff arrived later to tell me that Mother wanted me arrested! Because I had no prior history of violence, they only handed me a subpoena for a court hearing.

When the court date came up, I was shocked that all my family, except for my middle sister, testified that I went inside Mother's home and began beating her up, in the house. As the judge asked what happened, Mother explained it all. The Judge asked Mother, who hit who first? That was the one thing Mother could not remember.

The Judge looked at me and asked me what happened. I explained, that this woman had been using me as her personal punching bag my entire life and I was tired of her thinking she can hit me whenever she wanted.

The Judge asked me, "who hit whom first?"

I answered truthfully; "Mother hit me first."

The case was dismissed.

Again, I stopped speaking with Mother.

Loryel, Lauryn and I always shared an immense bond. At a very early age Lauryn would cry with such intensity when she was near others, even her own father, but not with me or her sister. It was as if our love created an unconditional bond that would last eternally. That is when Loryel and Lauryn became known as LoLa, a combined nickname for both my daughters.

When it was time for Loryel to enter high school, I feared having her going to a bad High School, as it was filled with gangs and seemed out of control. We spoke about it and I asked Loryel if she wanted to stay at her grandmother's during the week, and home on the weekend. Loryel thought it would be okay. So we completed the paperwork for Loryel to go school in Calvert County. Every Sunday evening, I would take Loryel, along with her groceries for the week to Mother's.

In no time, Loryel begged to come back home. So, I completed the paperwork and home Loryel came, and right to bad high School. By this time Lauryn was 3 years old, and life began to change. We suffered quietly as Anthony started being abusive. I was ashamed and kept it to myself but, yes, it was at this time that I began to really see that the man I lived with was a cheater and a drunk. He was losing jobs but going out every weekend with his friends, including my own brother. I had enough and finally kicked him out until he got himself together. Of course, Mother gave him a room to stay in at their house in DC.

After about a year or so, I thought he was doing better and slowly let him back into the condo with the girls. Little did I know, he began to become abusive to my girls, but threatened them not to tell me. When I asked him to leave again, he began breaking everything and punching holes in the wall.

I grabbed the girls and tried to lock us in our room but I had Lauryn in my arms and could not close the door in time. I had Loryel dial 911 as he grabbed my neck and told me that he was going to kill all three of us, as he had nothing to lose! The police showed up and told him he needed to leave, so Anthony packed a bag and left.

Then came the God awful day of 9/11/2001, the day of the attack on the World Trade Center Towers. Not long after verifying that my family in New York City was okay, I got the call that my grandmother, Elvira, had been found on the street and suffered a stroke and was in the hospital. Mother left first to go see her, and then we all followed. Unfortunately, my grandmother died on 9/25/2001. I took the girls and we went to New York City for my grandmother's funeral. It had been a while since I had seen much of the family, but I did learn that Mother was always in contact with them. It was great to see my uncles and my aunts. The girls never got to see their great grandmother, because we never knew where she was. As I was never included in family events, I was never told when family visited or even where any family members lived. My girls knew very little of my extended family, so they met their great grandmother at her funeral, along with my aunt and uncles. Many people approached me there and asked if I was the granddaughter of my grandmother? The more I replied that yes I was, the more people told me that I was beautiful and that I looked just like my grandmother. It was very comforting and it made me feel good that people I had never met saw my grandmother in me. Reacting to the compliments, two of my sisters began whispering behind my back and putting me down, saying to themselves, who I thought I was, distracting the attention from Grandma to me.

As mother always kept me away from majority of our family, I never knew when family would visit. If it wasn't for my grandmother's funeral, I would have never seen or even known that my uncles and my aunt were still alive.

It was actually my Aunt Jane, who happened to be a recovering heroin addict, who first warned me about Anthony's addiction. My aunt told me the signs to look for and to think about how much money he spent and whether his nose bled. I looked at bank statements and looked for the signs and they were dead on. In looking at the bank statement I noticed he would put in his paycheck and then take out more than he put into our account.

I also discovered that my own family knew about Anthony's cheating as well as his drug habit. My own family chose to protect my husband instead of their own daughter and sister. Despite his negative actions and threats against us, I did not want my daughter to live without her father. I did everything I could to provide supervised visits with Lauryn as I filed for custody and divorce. Anthony tried everything to stop the divorce, but I had made up my mind; my kids came first.

One day I came home from the store and left the girls in the condo. Anthony must have thought we were all gone. He climbed up three floors and removed the balcony door to get into the house. He was startled to find Loryel standing there, looking at him. He made Loryel promise not to tell me. Another time when the girls were at a friend's house and my little brother and I came home from the movies, I opened the door and there was Anthony, sitting on my couch with a knife in his hand. He thought I would be alone and my brother startled him. As I started to pull out my cell phone to call the police, he said "No, don't. I'm leaving." After he left, my brother pulled another butcher knife from the couch. It was clear that Anthony had been planning on killing me that night but didn't because I was with my brother. I walked into the kitchen, in complete shock and that is when I noticed, all the telephone lines had been ripped out of the walls. He had my murder all planned out.

A friend came over the next morning, to make sure all was okay, only to find Anthony waiting outside as if he had not broken into my home to kill me the night before.

Anthony got out of his car, and in front of my girls began attacking my friend. The attack stopped as quickly as it began, and he got into his car and drove off. He didn't love me; he just wanted to control me. I got the girls into the car and took them to their respective schools and went to work, only to find him waiting for me in the parking lot. Anthony began to stalk me and watch me as I would arrive to work. The year Lauryn started Kindergarten was the worst year of my life. Lauryn never cried when I walked out the door, dropping her off at school, but by mid noon, the teacher would call me, every day because Lauryn was crying. She thought for sure that Anthony would find me and kill me. Lauryn was so scared that I had to leave work to go pick her up.

That was the final straw. I went straight to the commissioner to file a restraining order to keep him away from my home, Lauryn's school, my job and the three of us in general. Our Divorce decree required supervised 2 hour visits, every other weekend, with security guards to protect us. Anthony also had to provide toxicology reports to prove he was drug free. Since the divorce, he provided two reports and nothing further. It never changed. Every time I called to have Lauryn speak to her father, he would ask for me. Each time he cursed me out and blamed me for the hell that he was going through. His support was $220.00 a month but Lauryn was lucky to see $120.00 a month. I created a post office box specifically for Anthony to be able to send Lauryn anything he wanted. It breaks my heart to say that he never sent anything.

Through all this, I started dating a man and we started getting closer, and the girls seemed to like him. He was married but told me he was in the middle of leaving her. As time passed, I believed him as he did move out. I thought he was great! I had known him since high school. By this time, I was not really speaking with my family, as I was still mad at the fact that they betrayed me and kept such pertinent information about Anthony being a drug addict, a secret.

It was at that time that Loryel and I decided to do whatever we needed to do to keep Lauryn happy and be there for her. We developed traditions and often took trips to the beach and for fun. I went nowhere without my girls and they went a lot of places, together. You could not ask for a greater love than the three of us had. As time passed, we also got closer to James as he started to join us and we often took road trips. We began to meet his family and I thought that he was a really good person to have around. He became close to the girls and won over Loryel as he helped her get her driver's license behind my back.

After some time, he began coming over often and after a year or so, he started staying over. After about two years he asked me to marry him. He went and asked my parents for their blessing and took me on a trip to Puerto Rico to propose.

It wasn't long before my youngest sister began lying to my fiancé. For some reason, she felt the need to tell him that I was a liar and that a friend from high school, who often called me, was actually my boyfriend. Why my sister would lie about something as stupid as that, I have no idea. I spoke with my parents and explained that this had to stop. They really needed to tell their children to stop bullying me. I decided, again, to stop speaking to them. My fiancé and I planned on getting a larger place my renting out my condo to a friend of mine.

Unfortunately, soon after we moved into the townhouse, I noticed things changing. His aunt was hit and killed by a truck and the family flew the body to their home country, for burial. I was not surprised that he did not want me to fly with him, as I trusted him. *BOY, WAS I WRONG!* As soon as he got back there were secret calls, late night talks and multiple trips back to his country. It was not long before I found out his entire family was lying to me. They all knew about his affairs. I found his secret phone with messages. One evening I popped over to his uncle's home and sure enough, there he was with his girlfriend, hugging, kissing and dancing. I confronted him as I walked behind them. He begged me to forgive him and stay but he wanted me to know that he did want to be with other women too. He wanted me as his wife but he wanted to have girlfriends too.

As soon as he left for work, I rented a truck. I packed my entire belongings and placed them into storage. My friend, allowed me to stay with her until I got my own place. The girls enjoyed it as it was a farm with the horses. I was grateful for her help.

I could not move back into condo because I had rented it to another friend. I let my friend know the situation and explained that I would have to increase the rent a little as I could not afford to pay the HOA fees, which I was going to pay for before the split. That friend never replied to me or let me know she was moving. She stole my special Corian cutting board that matched my kitchen counter and left my condo a mess. I even thought of suing her, but, then I decided to take the higher road, as always.

After a little while, I was able to find a place and the girls and I moved again. No sooner that we moved, I decided to go on my first vacation, ever, to Spain with some friends. It was relaxing and I really enjoyed it. My luggage arrived on day five out of my seven day stay but it was fun nonetheless and we really enjoyed ourselves. I returned home and I saw my ex-fiancé a few times but decided to leave him alone. I realized that I hated nothing more than a lying, cheating piece of shit! My girls and I were much better off without him, so good riddance.

Loryel was great and had her own car and was in college at this time. I loved all her friends and so did Lauryn. My girls were always together and I loved how good they were to each other. I never let my girls fight. I vowed NOT to be like my mother and required my children to treat each other with absolute respect. I had spent my entire life being abandoned, abused, molested, bullied, neglected and disrespected by my family and I was going to start standing up for myself. The only good thing about living 55 miles away from my family is that they NEVER visited me, unless they needed something. In contrast, my parents were always visiting my sister who lived nearby. My girls began to take notice and would always ask why they never visited them, as they were grandchildren too. As a matter of fact, Loryel was Mother's first grandchild, but the only grandchild who mattered was the one born to her and her husband's first born daughter.

They would call my children and ask them if their fingers were broken since they couldn't seem to call their grandparents. My girls would get upset, but I would defuse the anger and tell them to ignore them. We began to get settled in and enjoyed the new place. Lauryn was always with Loryel and hanging out but it was at this time that the darkness would linger back around. It hurt me to see that the only time that my children were seen by my family, was when I drove 55 miles to see them. If I did not drive to their house, they would never see my children. In order not to allow my kids to see my torment, I kept the darkness to myself. I was not sad, but I was ashamed that my own family went out of their way to be cruel to me. I wondered if this bothered my girls. I wondered if they could see my pain. I loved my daughters with every fiber in body and I just could not understand why my own mother hated me so much to purposely cause me pain. I often cried, when my girls went to sleep. I would shake it off, again, to concentrate on the girls, so were going out and having fun and nothing made me happiest but to see my girls so happy. I drove Lauryn to school and picked her up as I wanted to make sure that she was okay. Some months later, in November, 2007, an escaped convict managed to get out of the Hospital and there were police everywhere. I had one stop me and advise me that I should stay inside as there was an escaped convict with a gun. I told him I was okay and he gave me his card. He asked that I call him to make sure the person was caught. After work and on the way home, I called and sure enough the person had been caught. At this time the officer, John, asked me out for coffee. I told him I would think about it. Not too long after, I called back and agreed to coffee and to dinner. He was a good guy and we dated for a while before I thought I would introduce him to my girls.

I got a good feeling from this guy, because he really loved his German Boxer, Oskar. After several months John started to come over to visit with my girls and our dog, Precious. In no time we became inseparable. I had another friend, who was also a cop check him out, and he gave John the thumbs up and verified that it was okay to date him and start new paragraph.

I was still trying to allow Anthony to be a part of Lauryn's life. Lauryn had her own cell phone but she didn't want to give her father her number. We always used my phone for them to speak. No matter how much time went by, it was always the same thing. I called and I would hand Lauryn the phone and tell her to enjoy the call and if he asked about me, she should tell him I was not nearby. I had to do that because any time he spoke to me, he would yell and tell me how bad he was doing and that it was my entire fault.

Lauryn suffered badly from nose bleeds because her allergies were so bad. As a result, her nose to be cauterized in order to build up the interior layers in her nose and cover the exposed veins. After having Lauryn tested, she had to receive injections as Lauryn was allergic to just about everything in the environment, some foods and bees. I kept epinephrine on hand at all times, at home and at school. Lauryn loved getting on the back of John's motorcycle, and we went for family rides. Lauryn was so full of life and love. She loved school but at times, the fact that she was shy was hard. I spent some time sending emails or showing up for conferences as I did notice that Lauryn was the child teachers would take their aggression out on. Other children were out of control and were disrespectful, but not Lauryn. I often felt Lauryn's respect for them made it easier for teachers to yell at her. When Lauryn came home with this feeling of being bullied by her teachers, I made sure to meet with each teacher and let them know, I would not stand for my daughter to be their pin cushion. A lot of them apologized and Lauryn would be happy again.

As time went on and Lauryn grew, so did her beautiful personality. She loved so many things and enjoyed her life. Lauryn had to get braces, as her baby teeth would not come out and all but two had to be surgically removed. By the time she was in middle school, Lauryn required glasses too. We went shopping for her glasses. I worked hard to make sure that my girls received nothing but the best. It was around this time that Lauryn was diagnosed with Anemia!

As John, the girls and I got closer, and our blended family (of dogs) began, Loryel hung out with us a lot, even though she was in college. It did not bother me that she hung out so much, as I was always in fear that Anthony would find us, so I was very over protective. John, Lauryn and I had so many things we enjoyed doing. Riding motorcycles, hanging out, seeing movies, and at times Lauryn would ask to spend time over with some friends. After speaking with the parents, I had no issues with Lauryn going over to her friends' homes.

Loryel then found out she was pregnant. I was concerned that she had not completed college, but glad she had graduated from high school. Loryel prepared to move into her boyfriend, home. His parents allowed them to live in the basement of their home. Liha was born January 24, 2009, two days before Lauryn's birthday. Lauryn vowed that this was the best birthday gift ever! We had a lot of fun with Liha, and I was proud to see that Hector and Loryel were great parents. It was great to have Liha visit, as the dogs stood like statues around her. It was at that time I learned more about my dogs, as they became more vocal and it was all because of Liha. They did not like if Liha cried, so they would bark, continuously, until we attended to Liha. It was so comical and our home was full of so much love.

I noticed that no one came over to see Liha from my family, not even Mother! The darkness had its way of showing me things. Liha was now officially the first great grandchild to Mother and still, nothing. John and I watched as Loryel would drive to her grandmother's house on the weekend, so that they could see Liha. Loryel never seemed to catch on that she was doing exactly what I had done for many years; she was taking my granddaughter to see her great grandmother, 55 miles away.

John saw the pain my family caused me and could feel the negative energy so he never visited their home after the first time. John was the first person, in my life, whom my family could NOT manipulate, turn against me and control. I began to realize that there was finally a light through my darkness and there was still hope for a better future. I always suffered from kidney stones and Lauryn was always helping me through my difficult times, making sure that I was okay and when I was in pain, Lauryn would lie in the bed with me as I went to sleep. The majority of the time, I kept the pain to myself so that Lauryn would not worry so much.

As time passed, once again I forgave my family's ways and took Lauryn to visit. It was not long before another incident happened, however, so I was always prepared for another family attack on Linda's life. Loryel came to tell me that after all these years she found her father. I have never had an issue with Loryel's father, so I was fine with that, but Loryel was shocked that I was okay. About a week passed and both my girls came to me crying. It seems that Loryel hadn't searched for her father. Although it has never been a secret and I told Loryel I would help her find him, it was my sister who decided to take it upon herself to do the research and find my daughter's father. My sisters, mother, brother and stepfather – the whole family - decided to reach out and call Loryel's father, as well as friend him on Facebook, and then tell Loryel. Was I shocked? Yes, especially since Mother beat the crap out of me for asking for about my own father as a child. *So let me get this right; it was a crime to know my biological father but it was okay for them to go behind my back and find my daughters father.*

*Next* my girls began to tell me how my family would say horrible things about me when they spent the night there. They would tell my girls lies in order to make them turn against me. It was at that time, that my girls finally understood the pain I suffered in silence. For years the girls would return home and would be angry at me but I never knew why. After a couple of days, I would ask my girls what the problems and ask why they were being rude and it was as if a light went off in their heads. It was like they would wake up and realize it was me. My girls would always apologize and tell me they loved me, but never stated why they were mad in the first place. That was the last straw as far as John was concerned. John said he never wanted to see any of them again except for my middle sister. He would not stand there and smile in their faces, knowing how hateful my family was towards the girls and me.

The girls and I did many things together - bowling, shooting bows and arrows, knives, grappling, jiu-jitsu, Krav Maga, sports, games and shopping. Lauryn enjoyed taking photos and we were always doing things with our dogs. Lauryn loved animals and even had a parakeet, which she argued with every single day.

***

I kept the family at arm's length and attempted to stay to myself, which was working pretty well until a sister started to call me because she was concerned about her hair. As we were only half-sisters (I am full Puerto Rican) and only shared the same mother, we had different hair. The sisters have coarser hair and therefore had to get perms to get their hair straight. Since this sister had been getting perms since she was a child, her scalp suffered and she was forced to stop getting perms, so she called me because she was curious as to what she needed to do in order to heal as well as maintain healthy hair and scalp. My girls and I only used WEN hair products so I explained the reasons why. I also bought some WEN hair products for her, as well as other products to assist her on this journey. I also advised that she needed to try multiple products before she could figure out which was best for her hair.

This sister thought WEN was too expensive as only her boyfriend was working, so she could take care of their twins. I explained that in order for her to verify which product was better for her hair; she should use her PC and record a video of herself. I explained that way she could record the product, the process and the results. I also provided blogs so that she could see what I meant, when I explained how to record her videos. It just so happens that I had left on vacation so I told my girls that I'd ordered some WEN products for this sister and to let her know when they arrived. As this sister created the videos and began to enjoy testing the products, I told her she should create her own blog so that others can learn from her experience. So she did. I continued to advise and support this sister as she noticed others were reading her blogs. I was excited and happy for her for embracing her natural hair after she claimed the rest of the family told her hair looked bad and that she should perm it again.

There came a time that another blogger reached out and asked her to co-host a natural hair event in Virginia. She was excited and asked me to please come to the event and so I did!

As the event got closer, I was going through another kidney stone phase and I was very sick. I already had a kidney infection and I was in excruciating pain. Lauryn usually went everywhere with me, but she did not want to go to this event so I went alone as I did not want to let my sister down. I drove from Maryland to Virginia to support her. When I got there she introduced me to everyone and one of our cousins was even there. I always had long hair but wore it curly the majority of the time. It had been years since I flat ironed or used curlers in my hair and my girls were the same way.

During the event many people approached me and asked what I used in my hair and told me how beautiful I was and how gorgeous my hair was. I explained that I used WEN but that is not one of the products at this event. I advised that they should go to my sister, as she uses and knows the products at the event. There were a few people who questioned whether we had the same parents and I answered *"No, we do not, but we share the same mother"*.

As I was already hurting to attend this event, my pain got worse. I needed to leave the event so I said my goodbyes to my sister and our cousin. After the event my sister called to thank me for attending the event and I expressed how happy I was that she found joy with natural hair. A couple of days later, my sister sent an email to everyone in the family stating that she no longer wanted anyone to attend any of her hair events. She also stated that she did not appreciate her thunder being stolen after all her hard work and to keep away from anything that she did. Well, since I was the only sister who attended the event, I was confused as to why she would send such an email to our entire family. How did I steal her thunder? I was not there long! It just never stopped. All I did was be a good and supportive sister and I was made out to be a monster. Do you want to hear the funny part? After this rant about stealing her thunder and never wanting any more family at her events, she invited and took another sister to the very next hair event.

As she was sending out hate messages about me going to her event, I was in the hospital with 4 kidney stones with one cutting its way out. For the next two months Lauryn had to watch me go in and out of hospitals having multiple Lithotripsies' and one surgery to remove the stones. She also had time to read my emails, which Lauryn shared with Loryel. This was the last straw and my girls decided to take a stand against the family. As I concentrated on becoming healthy again, my girls began their planning. They spoke in detail about all the lies and all the things that my family had ever said to them. The girls decided to try one thing and that was to speak with their grandmother. At the birthday for my sister's daughter in July, 2012 the girls both expressed how badly we had been treated. They told their grandmother how they had been ignored and never treated like the rest of the grandchildren. Loryel pointed out that her grandmother idolized her grandson (who is 9 years younger than Loryel). Loryel expressed how she was the first grandchild and wanted to know why they never visited us, as they drove near our home almost every day of the week. Why did she allow her children to be so cruel to their mother? Why didn't she visit Liha, her first great grandchild? Why did we always have to go to them to visit? The girls told their grandmother that if she did not change and start acting like a mother and their grandmother, they would stop speaking to all of them.

The girls left that day thinking that there was no way their grandmother would ever change. It was at this time the darkness began to take its place in Lauryn's mind. We were not invited to family barbeques or family events and we were treated as if we were strangers. We were never called when other family members came to visit. It did not take long for the next evil act, and this time it was against my Lauryn, my 14-year-old daughter. My sister, went into Lauryn's Instagram account and pulled pictures and began texting and spreading them to other family members and gossiping that Lauryn was gay. My grown, thirty plus-year-old sister with four children, one was a teenager also, began gossiping about her own niece. When my youngest sister called to tell me what she was doing, I was floored. I felt my heart come out of my chest. I could care less about my child's sexuality! It was my child's health and happiness that I worried about. I had unconditional love for my daughters.

I called Loryel and John and told them what happened and we decided to be honest and tell Lauryn. When Lauryn got home, we told her that we would like for her to block everyone from her Instagram and mark it private. We also informed her of what her aunt was doing and how all of them were in on it.

John spoke up and looked at Lauryn and said, "We love you, and we are not asking you to speak about such a private matter until you are ready. As long as you are happy and are a good person and going to school, we are happy."

By this time my nephew began calling, texting and sending messages to Lauryn. We never really found out what he wanted, but we all knew that Lauryn hated him. We thought that there was a link between him, his mother and the rumor of Lauryn being gay.

My youngest sister was manipulative, as she kept calling and acting as if she didn't do anything wrong. Really! I had been a forgiving person my entire life. I had been molested, abused, neglected, abandoned, placed in foster care, disrespected, had false charges filed on me, placed in jail... and all this by my own mother and family! I was done. I saw the anger and rage take control of Lauryn and I decided to promise her that she would never see any of them ever again!

Lauryn looked at me and said "I would rather die than to see any of them ever again!" After months of having selected her new shotgun, for skeet & trap shooting, I went to buy Lauryn's shotgun only to discover that because of the old theft charge from my step brother, my shotgun application was denied. I was still listed with an indictment in Georgia. John had to buy the Franchi shotgun for Lauryn, as I was still considered a criminal.

Lauryn cried and just could not bear anymore. The people she thought were supposed to love and be loyal were the people who had tortured and bullied her mother and now her! Lauryn would cry and wonder how God could be so cruel. It was at that time I decided to take Lauryn to meet Mrs. Smith, my foster mother. During our visit, Mrs. Smith told Lauryn she looked exactly like me, when I was a teen. After our visit, Lauryn hugged me and thanked me for being so strong and for being such a great mom. I took this time to let Lauryn know that no matter what, I would always be there for her! I tried everything that I could to help Lauryn but could see the anger continue to build in her eyes. To make things worse, my sweet Lauryn went from being an honor student to having her grades slip dramatically. I reached out to the teachers but received no replies or assistance. I called the counselor, but she was not available. I continued to reach out, especially after receiving a letter on Lauryn's grades, until I got Lauryn's counselor on the phone. The counselor had no idea who my child was and automatically judged my daughter as lazy. It took everything I had NOT to curse this woman out. It was the job of the counselor to meet all their assigned students. School started 8/23/2012 and it was now five months later, and the counselor had never even met my daughter. I felt like it was being chastised for reaching out to her and she told me my daughter needs to get grades together. I had to force the counselor to at the portal to confirm and I'm sure the straight A's got her attention. I begged this counselor to call Lauryn down that day, and she said she would. I sent Lauryn a text to let her know the counselor was going to call her down and I told her to be honest and let the counselor know what was bothering her. Lauryn was so happy and texted me back to let know she was going to be honest because she can't take this anymore. As soon as Lauryn got home and I asked how it went, with a very sad face, Lauryn looked at me and said, "She never called me down." I kept my cool and decided to call and I left a couple of messages with NO return call from this counselor.

I decided to concentrate on Lauryn's birthday and asked her what she wanted to do? Lauryn said that she wanted to have some friends go rock climbing, so I said okay. I told Lauryn to invite whomever she wanted. The day before, we celebrated Liha's birthday and enjoyed our time with Hector (Liha's dad) and his family and friends. The next day, Lauryn's birthday, there was only one friend going, so I picked up Lauryn's friend, and off we went. We enjoyed the climbing and Lauryn seemed happy. We all went home and hung afterwards with pizza. I thought we finally were going to be okay, but then Mother sent Lauryn a Happy Birthday text three days after Lauryn's birthday. Lauryn was furious that this woman couldn't even remember her own granddaughter's birthday. Lauryn screamed how much she hated them all and made the same statement: *"I would rather die than to ever see any of them ever again."* I began to cry and held Lauryn. I promised again, that we would never see them again. We were moving and we would change our numbers. Lauryn said no, don't change the numbers that we will just block them from sending her anything.

Lauryn was clearly angry all the time. On February 15, 2013, after attempting unsuccessfully to speak with Lauryn about what was bothering her and trying to get her to open up, I gave her a hug and kiss and told her she needed to release all the penned up anger and talk to me. Lauryn lay down and took a nap for a little while that day. I needed to run an errand and asked Lauryn to come with me. Lauryn asked if she could stay home and asked me to buy her female products and something to eat.

I was gone about 35 minutes and as I walked back into the house, I was shocked by the sight of my daughter hanging, lifeless. I immediately cut Lauryn down and began CPR. As I was doing CPR, I grabbed the house phone to dial 911. The paramedics finally arrived and Lauryn's heart was still beating so they placed her on the gurney and sped off to the Regional Hospital. I tried to call, John but I could hardly speak, so the police informed him of what was happening.

John is a detective. He rushed home as his supervisor, other county police and the major consoled me in the hospital. Lauryn was stabilized and being sent by medevac to Johns Hopkins Pediatric Unit. The doctors let me see Lauryn so that I could kiss her and hold her before they took her from me. The doctor hugged me and told me that I saved her and that my quick CPR action was heroic.

As John went home to care for the dogs and make sure they were okay, a friend drove me to Johns Hopkins in Baltimore, Maryland. John had my phone and called my family to the hospital. Despite the fact that I only spoke with one sister, John called them all. Once John was done calling them he went through Red Cross to have Loryel pulled from Army Basic Training. The hospital did a great job to care for my sweet angel and I am forever thankful. I was able to sit with Lauryn and I just started to talk to her. As I cried and hugged my daughter's lifeless body I had to tell her "I love you princess and I forgive you. I will never be angry but I accept your decision and will find a way to be strong." Even though Anthony had never done anything but hurt my daughter, John used the arrest records to find his actual address to have him come see Lauryn.

I was not in a good place and I hated my family but I maintained my anger as I knew in my heart, they were the reason my daughter hung herself. After all Lauryn did say "I would rather die than to see any of them ever again." TWICE! My middle sister finally arrived and she went in the room with me and we lay with Lauryn. The nurses explained to me that Lauryn's heart might give out and they asked me if they could resuscitate. I said yes. At 4:09 a.m. on February 16, 2013 Lauryn's heart stopped and my heart broke! I could only cry. I loved my baby and could not understand why God allowed my daughter to kill herself!

To be honest I really cannot remember much! John did everything for me. John called my boss and began arrangements. John made sure Loryel was pulled and sent home. Loryel arrived on February 17, 2013 and we lay in bed as John held us and gave us medicine to have us sleep. As we all want to be donors and be cremated, John reached out and we verified to have Lauryn be a part of the Donate Life through the Living Legacy Foundation. There were a lot of people visiting us, in and out to include Lauryn's God Father, who Lauryn never saw again when he married his wife. During this horrible time you'd think there was nothing worse that my family could do, right? WRONG! Loryel and I began to go through Lauryn's room and we decided to donate some of her things and we also selected some friends to receive some of Lauryn's personal belongings. We began slowly gathering everything in her room. John took us to the funeral home to make preparations for a service and we selected an Urn for us and we even picked a smaller Urn for Anthony. The day came for the service, so Loryel and I rode with John. The police psychiatrist was a constant since the hospital, and he helped us a lot. I was a mess and there was nothing that Loryel and I wanted except to go home. As soon as we got home, the investigating detectives found some notes that Lauryn had written and presented them to us. I was not surprised to find notes saying how much she loved her Mom, Sissy, Liha, John, our dogs and her bird. I was not surprised to see how much she hated my parents, siblings and cousins. I was surprised that Lauryn wrote "I hate being a part of the most heartless family." I was so upset to see that message because had I known, I would have never have had any of my family at Lauryn's service.

I'm sure by now you just know that there is nothing more that my family could do to hurt us. WRONG! Again, my family somehow got a hold of Loryel's friend's cell phone numbers and started spreading more lies and rumors that Lauryn did NOT commit suicide but that John killed Lauryn and I was covering it up. Mother kept showing up at my door, as if I needed her for anything. We kept asking her to stop coming, and that I didn't need her. "It's your entire fault!" I told her, "All of you! All you need to do is tell your children to stop being cruel and mean to me and my kids!"

Wouldn't you know that evil sister decided to blog about Lauryn's death and how much she was hurting? The witch wrote how her heart was broken and she did not know how to deal with her grief. Sure, post my daughter's death all over your paid blog sites and websites to get more viewers and followers. Loryel sent that sister an email asking her to please take down the blog. She responded and said she was going to sue Loryel for harassment and asked Loryel where she was when Lauryn was dying in the hospital? "I was the one comforting your mother and NOT YOU!" that sister went on to say, "Where were you, Loryel?"

We promised Lauryn she would never have to see any of them again and that is exactly what we are doing - never seeing them, ever again!

I lived with such darkness inside me and I never even had to tell Lauryn of my darkness; she felt it. My poor daughter not only empathized with everything I grew up with, but also endured my family doing the same to her. Lauryn suffered with the darkness and did not let me know of her suicidal thoughts. I had no idea some of her friends had been institutionalized and suffered from depression. Lauryn's darkness grew and in fear that she too, would be institutionalized, the darkness won and the Silent Killer got its way. The Silent Killer lives in us all and it begins as rage and sorrow. Lauryn hid her darkness from me because she thought I had enough to worry about and she needed to spare me more darkness.

Now I fight the Darkness to expose The Silent Killer. I have become an advocate to spread awareness of depression as well as the prevention of suicide through the Out of the Darkness Walks. I reach out to children in trouble and educate parents on how to better understand our children. I help children to better communicate with their parents. As the schools in my district are not doing anything or providing guidance for our children, I will fight to help them! The children need to believe that there are people who care and we can help! I will never give up as long as there is always HOPE.

http://lauryn-santiago.virtual-memorials.com/

If you know anyone living with Mental Illness, the following are resources that will assist. Please do not allow others to suffer alone. Please help.

The Centers for Disease Control and Prevention (CDC) collects data about mortality in the U.S., including deaths by suicide. In 2013 (the most recent year for which full data are available), 41,149 suicides were reported, making suicide the 10th leading cause of death for Americans In that year, someone in the country died by suicide every 12.8 minutes.

National Suicide Prevention Lifeline: 1 (800) 273-8255  **Hours:** 24 hours, 7 days a week

**Languages:** English, Spanish
**Website:** www.**suicideprevention**lifeline.org

American Foundation for Suicide Prevention
http://afsp.org/

Your Life Matters (UMTTR)
http://www.umttr.org/

The Campaign to Change Direction
http://www.changedirection.org/

# VIRTUE
## Receive Mercy and Find Grace- By Norra Prescott

"I cannot believe that bitch has been sleeping with my husband."

This is my only thought. My thought is not, "I cannot believe that asshole slept with my sister-in-law." Well, we always blame the woman, but in all honesty I never liked her.

"At least she is pretty," I think with tears in my eyes. Usually they cheat with the first skank willing to open her legs, like that white chick he met in reception -a hooker type looking trick in short skirts with fake nails and hair and three very real children who spent the night with her Baby Daddy when they were together. He confessed to me later that she meant nothing that she was just available when I wasn't, that our twin boys were overwhelming for him and she listened to him. She was there for him. She had no strings or ties and would oblige him in any way. She offered freedom from the stress I gave him with the bills, the children, and the responsibility.

So I forgave him! I took him back into our home, our family, my heart, and my bed. So, of course, I get pregnant again. I am four months from delivering our long awaited baby girl – *my* long awaited baby girl - and I find out he is screwing my sister-in-law.

Nikki is gorgeous, childless, with a great job, a Master's degree and she has mastered fucking my husband. She has a great figure, big house, flat stomach and is fucking my husband. She is worldly, strong, and able to leap tall buildings in a single fuckin' bound and is fucking my husband.

I still remember Jeff's face when we first met her. My brother bought her to our family reunion. She wore a BCBG pale yellow sun dress, Arabella Coach sunglasses and Tory Burch sandals. She charmed them all in a way I could only dream of doing and my husband looked at her like a pork chop, and I am quite sure he ate her!

Jerome came over and said, "Jeff, Grace, this is Nikki." Jeff almost drooled. And I hated her. I hated her for pulling my husband's eye. I had caught him looking at other women but never like this - not as if he wanted to screw her, but as if he wanted to love her. Nikki was taken aback by his reaction to the introduction, but she dismissed it. She even dismissed Jeff's attempt to hug her when they left the party. I saw everything, even as I was attending to our one-year-old twins. Jerome was, of course, oblivious to all.

Jerome was too smitten to see anything. He just stuck out his chest like a king with this goddess on his arm. Funny, it did not look like love when Jerome looked at her. It looked like he owned her. He acted as if she was one of his possessions, like his black 325 BMW or his four bedroom condo in Arlington. She was just another thing to be proud of but not something to love.

I never told anyone what I saw in Jeff's face. I denied it to myself until I overheard him on the phone with her making plans to go to Florida for "business". I heard him making plans for the dinner they would have. I heard him making plans for her to wear a certain red bikini he was particularly fond of seeing her wear. And I heard him request that she bring his favorite green and blue lingerie and that she would perform her chair and pole show for him. I heard in his voice his longing for her and the passion he used to have for me; a passion that had been dead in our marriage for years.

When I met Jeff, he said I had the most beautiful smile he had ever seen. It is true. My smile is my favorite feature about myself. It still is when I can conjure it. I am a beautiful chocolate sister, and when I smile, all men (and some women) stop to admire my glow.

I knew Jeff was the one when I saw his eyes. They are honey brown, and I could see our daughters with his eyes and my smile. They would be beautiful, and there would be five of them.

I come from a family of four. I am the youngest girl; my parents and my older brother (the slut's husband). They all sheltered me.

We lost my father about four years ago. My father was my idol. He was an amazing man. He spoiled my mother. It is because of their example I believed I was not supposed to get divorced. I was supposed to get married and stay married like my parents. They had been married for 27 years by the time of my wedding. Talk about a standard to try to live up to!! I'd seen them argue, but never fight. They never slept in separate rooms. They always had dinner together, and my Dad bought gifts and flowers for my mother every birthday, Valentine's Day, and Mother's Day. For their anniversary, he would buy a rose to represent each year they were married and we would all go out to dinner at a fancy restaurant. My mother always drove the new car, parked in the single garage, and had the option to work. If there was ever any infidelity, it was never obvious to me or my brother. The four of us were a picture perfect family to the core.

So I am looking at my whoring husband wondering where I went wrong. This is not the first time he has been unfaithful, but this is the first time I have ever felt threatened. I feel he may really leave me, and the boys. His single other conquest was never serious, and I overlooked it. He swore he never cared for her and when I told him to stop seeing her; he did so without any argument. It just took two words: *child support.* So why does this feel so different? How did this floozy in Gucci come along and take my husband's affection and attention?

I've confessed to his infidelity; but have I told you of mine?

Dan was amazing. He had his own business. He was worth more than the home Jeff and I shared. And he was very married.

I was in graduate school, and he taught my business management class. There was something about his wealth that was undeniable. He wore tailored suits, Italian shoes and smelled of sandalwood and myrrh the way a man should.

I worked for him while earning my degree, and he told me my smile was like an angel singing and my skin was as soft as a child's.

I did not care that he was married. I did not care that he had two children at home. He made me feel worldly. He made me feel like a woman. He devoured my body and made love to my spirit. The only thing that kept me from falling in love with him was his wife.

The wife that would call just as his tongue flicked my clit to tell Dan that the baby needed formula. The wife that would interrupt our romantic dinner in Morton's private room to remind him that he had missed Timmy's tee ball game yet again. (Oh and by the way, Timmy scored the winning run).

Now, I know. I know that she knew his business meetings that ran until 10:00 p.m. were not business meetings, that working late until 2:00 a.m. had nothing to do with his accountant, that the hanging out with the fellas at the bar did not involve fellas at all. I know these excuses had everything to do with his being with me. I know because I heard them. I heard them then, when I was under him and I heard them when my husband offered them to me. Like Dan's wife, I accepted them because I had to. When you are sitting at home with a bottle of Pinot, and your husband is feeding you his excuse as to why he is not home to read the bedtime story to your three-year-old twins; you know why. So your question should not be, "What is he doing?" Your question should be," When have I heard this?"

Was I not the one sitting at the restaurant table listening while he told his wife he was dining with a client? I am certain that was me lying in the bed when his wife shrieked on the phone as to his whereabouts while he insisted he was working to a deadline for a proposal. Surely our vacation to Miami was excused under the guise of a business conference.
I stopped seeing Dan after our second Christmas together. He bought me a brand new black Honda Civic. I was thrilled. We walked into the dealership on Christmas Eve and there was a big bow accompanied with a huge "To/From" card. "To Grace: From Dan" it read. I was thrilled! We went home and made love all afternoon.

I wanted him to be with me Christmas morning. I had always loved Christmas and I thought there was something magical about us celebrating together. But he left. He left my home and my arms. He had bikes to pick up. He had to attend the Christmas service at church with his family. So I spent my Christmas Eve with no one to hug, kiss, or cuddle. This is the downside of being the other woman. You don't get to show your man at family dinners. You are not the one going to the office parties. You are not in the forefront.

The next day, as I was on my way to have dinner with my parents (I drove my old car because I was not up for the awkward questions), I drove by Dan's home. In the driveway was a brand new Mercedes with a big red bow and a big card that read "To: E.C; From: Dan". So, clearly, the other downside of being the other woman is the wife gets the better car. That was when I realized I no longer wanted to be the side woman. It works for some, but it was not the relationship I wanted. I am much too vain to be second choice.

Because of Dan, I am not surprised at Jeff's cheating. I expected it. That has always been my relationship with karma. She loves to show me the other side of my decisions. But was Jeff actually leaving me? Was Jeff actually thinking he could have a happily ever after with another woman? I chuckled slightly as I pondered that notion.

***

It was a few month after the first of the year when Dan and I broke up... or I should say, after I thought I should confront Dan's wife. After 14 months with him, I had had enough. I was tired of being alone. He had professed love to me and said he would leave her the first chance he got.

I thought I would help him with that chance. I went to Dan's home and rang the doorbell. His stay-at-home wife answered. I told her, "My name is Grace, and I am sleeping with your husband."

She replied, "Oh. My name is E.C, and who isn't?"

She eyed, my new Civic in the driveway and complimented. "Oh, you finagled a car out of the deal. The last one only got a pair of half carat diamond earrings. You must have mad skill; but none better than mine." This pronouncement was followed by a door slam.

At that point, I figured Dan and I were done.

I met Jeff four months after I confronted E.C. I frequented a Starbucks that was across the street from my office building. I was there at 7:30 a.m. each Tuesday and Friday before my standing Project Management meeting. I always got a Grande Skinny Hazelnut Latte Extra Hot. One Friday the barista told me that my drink was free. "The gentleman paid for your latte, ma'am", he told me.

"What gentleman?, I asked.

The barista looked around, but Jeff had gone.

This went on for two more Fridays. I was at the Starbucks at 6:45 a.m. to perform surveillance on my latte benefactor. I was in cahoots with the barista, who promised she would give me a signal when Jeff came in to place his and my order.

When he arrived, I thought he was the most beautiful man I had ever seen. He was fair skinned with hazel eyes. I saw visions of our life together. We would have three beautiful little girls that had my Hershey chocolate face with his hazel eyes.

He startled when the barista told him that his drink had been paid for. Then he turned to face me. I remembered the stopping of my heart immediately followed by a quickening. I was over Dan and any other man I had met before in that instant. I had never been a love a first site type of woman, but I really have no other way to describe my feeling.

He walked over to me. He had a slow sexy stride that made me gasp.

"Hello and thank you," he said.

I decided to let him know he was busted. "No, thank you. I wanted to meet my benefactor and it seems I owe you at least two more Black Pike Roasts."

"You don't owe me anything. Those were gifts for gracing me with your presence."

His voice! I thought I would melt. I managed to hold it together, but I blushed. "You do know how to inflate a girl's ego."

He glanced at my Jones New York form fitting dress as if that was not the only thing inflated.

We sat and talked until he asked me if I wanted to go out with him on Saturday. We exchanged numbers.

Just after my standing Friday meeting I got a text message from him: *"I do not want to wait until tomorrow to see you for dinner. Can we have lunch together?"*

I laughed and blushed so that my girls at work started to inquire. I told them about the weekly lattes and my sting operation to catch my admirer. We giggled and discussed my options.

"Don't go chasing after him," Tina suggested. I can only describe Tina as being a dude trapped in a woman's body. She felt men were meant to be at her beck and call. They were not people as much as instruments designed for her pleasure.

"No, you should accept. You can see if he is really worth your time," advised Donna, the hopeless romantic with a daughter by a married man and who refused to be thwarted on the idea of happily ever after.

In the end, I decided to play a little coy. I told Jeff I already had lunch plans and that this evening could not be arranged either. "Sorry, Saturday is all I have. But I will be worth it," I promised. There was no way I was going to let him start off controlling this relationship.

And I was. I hit the gym first thing that morning, scheduled my monthly massage immediately after, and scheduled a hair appointment with the Dominicans. I even bought a new dress, a knock off Michael Kors number I found at the Ross in McLean, Virginia. By 5:00 PM that Saturday, I looked fabulous.

We met at Bohemian Caverns on U Street in Washington DC. I felt like a queen as eyes turned to admire me as I sauntered across the room to meet Jeff. He looked as though he had just won the lottery; and that made me feel even better about the effort I'd put into my appearance.

We had a wonderful first date, but I have to confess, my thoughts frequently wandered back to Dan. Would I run into him? Would his wife be with him? Would he be jealous? I do not think of Jeff as my rebound guy, but I did miss the lifestyle Dan gave me. Dan bought me a car while Jeff bought bracelets. Still, I felt Jeff really loved me. He was certainly available to me in a way that Dan was not. Our breakup was sudden and I offered little in the way of an explanation. I simply felt I needed more and deserved better.

***

Jeff and I had a beautiful wedding. My only regret was that my mother was not alive to attend the wedding. She had been diagnosed with uterine cancer shortly after Jeff had proposed. Unfortunately, it was a very aggressive and by the time she was diagnosed, it was too late.

Jeff and I told her about the proposal while she was in the hospital. He was very attentive and teased the nurses and the doctors that they needed to make sure his mother got their undivided attention. She adored Jeff. She said he reminded her of my father; handsome and charming. As she said it, her face drifted off to a painful place, but she patted my hand and told me how lucky I was to have found him.

She died two days after that visit. Jeff and Nikki helped Jerome and I make arrangements. They had flown to Reno to marry. They had a large reception when they returned. I knew I did not want that to be my fate. I was going to be a bride. My dress would be so beautiful that I would look as though I was floating down the aisle. I would look like a Queen with my King waiting for me to live happily ever after.

We married on Cayman Brac where he proposed. We had gone there on vacation. It was a weekend excursion. We snorkeled, hiked, parasailed, and made such beautiful love. I loved him. He lived in my very soul. I lived for each beat of his heart. I watched him sleep. I prayed for his wellbeing. I wanted him to be happy with me above anyone or anything else. And I know I am the only one who can love him this way.

We moved into his townhouse in Vienna, Virginia. We settled into our routine. I went to work early in the morning so I would have dinner ready each evening. Jeff mowed the lawn Saturday mornings and made sure the bushes stayed trim. Jeff did dishes, and I did the laundry. We made love every night, so it should not have been a surprise when I found out I was pregnant.

I had been on birth control during the time we were dating. I expected that it would take more than three months for me to get pregnant. I expected that we would go to Hawaii. I expected that we would buy a house before we started a family. I was wrong on all counts.

I told Jeff on our monthly Friday date night. I was so scared to tell him, but he was thrilled. He jumped up in the middle of McCormick and Schmidt and started dancing and spinning me around. We ran to the closest Walgreens and bought five home pregnancy tests and four large liters of water. I drank water for the rest of the evening and peed on all five sticks. Every single one was positive and Jeff wanted to put them in a picture frame. I laughed and told him that was the grossest thing I had ever heard. His reaction once again was also not the one I had been expecting. Clearly, I should have not made any expectations about pregnancy.

Jeff attended every doctor's appointment with me. He actually saw the heartbeat on the sonogram before I did. Another issue was that now our three bedroom townhome was much too small. It was pretty obvious that in the very immediate future we need to buy a house. Some place with a big back yard in an area with a good school system. So, we put Jeff's townhouse on the market. My condo was being rented, and the tenants were solidly paying the rent on time. Jeff and I decided that we would sell that property if we needed the money for child care or school.

It was by God's grace that the townhome sold within the month. Jeff's maintenance on the yard made it very attractive for buyers. Unfortunately, our house hunting was not as successful. Jeff and I disagreed on style and size. Jeff wanted a home that had been lived in because he thought the house "kinks" would have manifested. I wanted something new and modern; a used house just made me feel like I was living off of someone else's memories. In the end, Jeff gave in, and we bought a brand new home.

Moving while pregnant was a very stressful time for us. I was moody and irritable. It was while I was packing that I started having very painful cramps and then I felt my water break. Oh no, I thought. I am only 5 months pregnant.

I prayed, "God, please no. "

I called Jeff from the basement he took one look at the water on the floor and my tormented face and he called Dr. Walker. She said she would meet us at the hospital. I grabbed a towel to sit on while Jeff drove to the hospital. It was soaked with blood by the time we got to the emergency room.

When we arrived, I was immediately admitted to the maternity ward and hooked up to the sonogram machine. The nurse looked at Jeff's anxious face and slowly shook her head. She never looked at me. She only communicated with Jeff. It was like she could not face me with the news. Tears ran down my face. I could not control them. My heart was broken.

I stayed in the hospital for two days. My baby had been a little girl. I wanted a little girl, one I could dress up and enroll in dance class. Every time I thought about my little girl I hit the morphine drip. Unfortunately, the morphine did nothing to cure my heart pain.

Jeff would not talk about it. He proceeded with the move into our new home insisting that having a new start could not have come at a better time. But he started staying out late; sometimes I would not see him until the next day. He reeked of smoke and liquor. Once when he came out of the shower I noticed scratches on his back. I was so deep in my grief that I did not even address it. We had not been married a year and we were already having problems. He was already having an affair. I lost a baby, his baby, and the only thing he could do was to stick his dick into another woman.

It was months before we had sex. I became consumed with having a baby. It was the only thing I thought about and the only reason I had sex. It seemed to take forever, but I got pregnant. I had lost my enthusiasm. I kept expecting to lose the baby; I just did not know when it was going to happen.

Jeff had lost his passion for our family. When I told him I was pregnant this time he just gave me a weak smile and a congratulatory kiss then left for the evening. He managed to come with me to my first appointment. When the doctor pointed out the second heartbeat, Jeff's face immediately showed worry.

"We are expecting twins?" he asked Dr. Walker.

She smiled at his concern and nodded. She assured him that he would be fine.

We were prepared to accommodate one baby, but not quite ready for two babies. All of our expenses would be doubled. Day care costs $13,000 a year for just one child. Plus there were the expenses of the diapers, food and clothes. We could rely on Jeff's parents to help with the child care, but his mother was in poor health and Jerome had his own life. My concern was whether or not I could rely on Jeff. He had been so distant since we had lost our daughter. He was out every evening from Thursday to Sunday. We did not go anywhere together. It was as if he could barely be in the same room with me. He treated me as though I had let him down. I had failed some test he had for me, so he was going to punish me by screwing around.

It hurt. I had life inside of me, and he was missing it. I was missing him. I was still in love with him. I was not going to stop loving him. He was my soul mate. God picked him for me, and I was not going to give up on this marriage and our family.

I delivered our twin boys after seven months of pregnancy. How beautiful they were. They were four pounds each born 3 minutes apart. Jeff was there and for the first time in over a year, he looked happy again. He looked as if he loved me. He looked the way he had on the day we married. I felt hopeful. I felt we would be a family.

It took about three months for Jeff to resume the Thursday through Sunday evenings out again. Nicholas and Jason slept, cried, ate, and crapped almost non-stop. It was like an endless cycle. We would get Nicholas straight and Jason would need something else. Jeff did at least bring diapers home, but he was almost non-existent in everything else. He cried stress.

Stress? For him? Stress? Stress was trying to take care of infants as a single parent. Stress was not being sure if you were supposed to feed the baby's butt or change his face.

When I returned to work after my maternity leave, I almost kissed my co-workers. The boys were beginning to sleep through the night and I had settled into a new routine. I had found that I could count on Jeff to watch the boys in the evenings during the week. His mother gave me relief for a few hours a month by letting me go to the spa to get a massage or a mani-pedi. (Love that woman!) I suspect she knew Jeff was not holding up his end of our marriage. I think she felt sorry for me. I had no shame in taking her pity. It certainly helped keep me sane.

One night when my mother-in-law had the boys, I followed Jeff. The woman I saw him with was total trash. She was short, heavyset and dressed in a very tight and short outfit. In all honesty it looked like she borrowed it from someone who was actually a decent size. It was strange but I felt better after I saw her. He was screwing trash. These were not women he would leave me to be with. They went to her house and I did a drive by during the week. She had three kids! Oh, he was definitely not going to leave me. Still, I never confronted him about his infidelity. I ignored it and buried myself in the life of my boys.

When they were three, Jeff actually decided to coach their soccer team. I was surprised, he had not so much as spent five unsupervised minutes with them. I encouraged this and he stopped hanging out in the evenings. He still did not seem to want to spend time with me. He was still so distant.

Jerome called late one evening saying he needed to talk to us. He and Nikki wanted to invite Jeff and me over for dinner. He said he had some news for us. There was an edge to his voice. I was not sure how to read his tone.

We got a sitter for the twins and I selected a Malbec for us to have. Nikki looked her usual ravishing self in a maxi-dress and her hair carelessly flowing over her shoulders. She had cooked a roast with rosemary potatoes, and it was delicious. The fact that she could cook made me detest her even more. Jeff went on and on about how good the meal was and about how lucky Jerome was to have Nikki. I almost gagged into my plate.

After dinner, Jerome said that he had a job offer in California. He was so excited. It was a startup company in Silicon Valley that would allow him to use his anti-hacking skills at some major corporate level. I barely understood what he did in general and I understood this even less; I could only pay attention to his enthusiasm to see this was an amazing opportunity for him. Nikki's reaction was the exact opposite of Jerome's. Where he was excited and exuberant, she was sullen and only drank the wine. She made no contribution to Jerome's bliss. In fact, her attitude was completely indifferent. When Jerome finally stopped talking, I congratulated them both and asked when they would be leaving. Jerome replied that he would have to fly out for a few months to get things started, set up meetings and make contacts. It was likely they would be moving in the next 6-8 months.

Nikki replied, "I'm not going. This is Jerome's job offer."

Jeff and I stared at her. Clearly, she and Jerome had had this discussion, and it seemed to go the way it was going in front of us. Now it was his turn to clam up like a shell and quietly drink his wine. My mind was reeling with questions. What was going on? Were Jerome and Nikki having marriage problems? Her family lived only a few miles away and her mother was in a home. I know she had a lot of close friends who lived in the area. She had, in fact, been in this area all of her life. But isn't that the reason they make plane tickets, so you can visit? Jerome had confided a few months before that they had trouble conceiving a baby, but was that a reason to end their marriage?

Something told me that was it. They were having difficulty conceiving. I knew firsthand what damage the loss of a baby could do to a marriage. If this was the problem, surely we could talk with them. Maybe we could help them; maybe they could help us. It was strange, but I felt very close to Nikki at that moment; her not being able to conceive and my losing that which was conceived. I still grieved for my daughter. I had never let that go. We were sisters in that moment; her husband being too selfish to care and my husband emotionally checking out so he did not have to care.

I have no misconceptions about my brother. He is a really nice guy, but when it comes down to it, he will save himself and to Hell with everyone else. He was spoiled as a child. He was the only child for five years. He tolerated me because I was a girl and did not interfere with his space. But he is selfish to the core. His wife was on the verge of broken. I could look at her and see she was barely holding it together, and he was going on about some startup venture.

I helped Nikki clean up that evening. While we were in the kitchen, I told her if she needed to talk, I was there for her. She looked at me as if I had grown a second head. She had obviously felt my dislike toward her. She thanked me for my concern and Jeff and I went home for the evening.

We did not discuss the evening. We stuck to friendly talk about the twins. We discussed the new clothes they needed, the upcoming childcare tuition, and how proud we were of them.

My mind was on Nikki and Jerome. I marveled at how alike my brother and Jeff were. I wondered if all men were this way, or if Nikki and I just hit the jackpot by marrying such similarly selfish men. I wondered about Dan. His actions were selfish also, and in hindsight, I should have expected more from myself. It belittled me to become involved with him. Did his behavior have the same impact on his family as Jeff's was now having on ours? I did not want to confront the fact that perhaps I would be the cause of distancing in a marriage. I did not want to face the fact that I was surrounded by people who did not seem to care about what happened when you only thought about yourself. I had done it when I was with Dan. Jeff and Jerome were doing it now. So I only discussed happy and safe things with my husband and wondered where his thoughts were; because I doubt he was as interested as he pretended to be in the boys' potty training.

It was during the Thanksgiving holiday when I realized how strained things were between Jeff and me. He was easily irritated with me. He would criticize that my dress was too plain or that I should color my hair.

I would rebut that he could use more visits to the gym during lunch instead of to the bar after work. I commented that he could concentrate on moving up at work so I could stop working and we could work on having my daughter. When I commented on his lacking career Jeff would become stoic. He never seemed to understand how much better he could be doing. He was finishing his Masters of Information Systems and he could easily be the director of his division and even VP of the Corporate Information Systems Division, but he was content to manage the four guys he had been managing for the last three years.

Our arguments were catty, and Jeff opted to just avoid being wherever I was. If the boys and I were upstairs, Jeff was in the basement. If I was in the kitchen, he would go to the family room and play with the twins. On occasion, he even found excuses to sleep in our guest bed room. He would declare, "Yeah, Babe, I had beans for lunch and I didn't want to offend you." Sometimes he would even opt to sleep on the sofa rather than next to me.

I was determined to be normal. Jeff and I had hosted the family Thanksgiving celebration since we had married. I refused to let his behavior deter me. I suspected he was again seeing someone, but this was the first time he had neglected me like this. We would invite our usual friends and family; his mother, Jeff and Nikki, and a friend of mine I had befriended at work, Sarah.

Sarah was widowed due to the negligence of a doctor. Her husband of 3 years had gone in to have a tumor removed from his lung. The doctor had a history of drug use and the hospital failed to detect his dependence. Her husband had a seizure during the surgery when he suddenly convulsed and the doctor stabbed her husband with his knife. She never went to court. She said her religion did not allow her to sue, but the hospital gave her a check for an undisclosed amount. Sarah believed this was God's grace because she did his will.

I liked her company because she was very sweet and calming for me. She was very active in her church and always had a passage for me when I found myself being tested; like then.

I made the turkey, stuffing, sweet potatoes, rice, collard greens and Mama bought her famous red velvet cake for dessert. Jerome was out of town in California, and his flight was delayed due to the excessive ice. It was early Thursday morning when he called to apologize to say he was not going to make it. Jeff called Nikki to tell her that she was still welcome to come. On the phone I practically heard him beg her not to stay home and miss the Thanksgiving dinner. She must have conceded because she was on our doorstep with 3 bottles of wine an hour and a half later.

Jeff greeted her and his attitude was buoyant from the time Nikki arrived. I felt as if they were hosting this affair and I was a guest. She taught songs to the kids and was just nauseatingly happy. She helped me in the kitchen. She helped me serve the food. She made sure each guest that had wine, tea, soda or water.

This was the event Jeff and I used to put up our Christmas tree. And it was Nikki and Jeff who spearheaded the Christmas Carols and the trimming of the tree. There is even a picture taken that year that shows Jeff holding Nick next to Nikki holding Jason, and I thought of how I resented Nick's name being so close to hers.

I was confused and heartbroken, and I was not entirely sure why. I knew Jerome was out of town. I knew Jerome and Nikki seemed to be having marital issues. I knew Jeff and I were having marital problems. And I knew that Jeff was attracted to Nikki. Things were clicking for me, but I ignored the clicks. I ignored my gut feeling. I ignored that my husband was falling or had fallen for Nikki.

After the party, I went into Jeff's messages. He was always too lazy to change the default message of the last 4-digits of his password login. There was a message from Nikki. *"Thank you for talking me into coming. I had a really nice time."* That was it! While I was holding the phone, a voice message came. Unfortunately, he did lock his cell phone. I played with the combinations and the password was the twins' birthday. It was Nikki again.

*"This between us cannot continue, but I do miss you,"* she said.

Jeff was asleep in the bed. I stormed upstairs and threw the phone at him.

"You are one sorry ass jackass!" I exclaimed. "You are fucking Nikki! You bastard! You sorry excuse of a man!"

He did not even try to deny it. He did not make any excuses. He just tried to block the picture frame, and other knick knacks that I hurled at him.

"She is my sister-in-law! How could you do this?" I raged as I flew at him with my fists. I was in flames. I was heartbroken. I had felt sorry for that bitch for losing her child. Now I wished she would be barren for the rest of her life. It was Jason who broke my tirade. I must have awakened him with my yelling.

"Mommy", he said simply.

I was beating Jeff with my fists when he saw us. Jeff had a cut on his arm. One of my targets must have been true.

I looked at him and said, "get out" as calmly as I could.

I grabbed Jason and kissed him and walked him back to his bed. I had to hold him all night and it was daybreak when he finally fell asleep. I heard the beep of the door and Jeff was gone.

### Nikki's Account

I should feel guilty for loving Jeff. Grace should have gotten the hint that she needs to be the wife and the mistress. She got so wrapped up in being the wife that she threw sexiness out the window. She is just like her brother, too caught up in the details. We work hard, we deserve excitement. Jerome and Grace are so stuck with the status quo. I loved Jeff from day one. Jeff stimulates my mind; he stretches my sexual fantasies beyond the status quo. It is magic. I love what he does to me; enough to say FUCK the world and everything that can be lost.

I was Jeff's dream. We talked all the time about running away. I told Jerome when we got married that Jeff made me feel uncomfortable. At our wedding, he was our best man. When he passed the ring to Jerome, I got chills. After the wedding, when we would see each other those chills became tingles in places that I cannot describe. I would walk around banging my head against the wall wondering why I felt he was so hot. I wondered why I did not feel guilty for wanting her husband.

"This is not high school" I would say to myself.

I thought about of the consequences of me acting on this crazy obsession with Jeff. I convinced myself I was just that- obsessed. I had to be crazy to be obsessing over a married man.

I even prayed for God to deliver me from wanting a married man. Please ignite my feelings for my husband instead of Jeff. I would do anything that I could to distract myself from dreaming about Jeff. I would sit with a glass of wine and watch Scandal. The lovemaking scenes caused me to imagine me and Jeff in the actor's places. I would change the channel to Disney channel, which made things worse because I would dream about me and Jeff raising a family together.

One day the universe responded to my desires. Jeff called me and asked me to lunch so that we could discuss partnering on a project for a client.

"Nikki, I can use the fact that you have a Master's degree to bid on this contract, can we meet today and talk over lunch at Clydes?"

My mouth filled and my body tingled.

"Yes. Jeff, I look forward to justifying the reason I have this Master's degree, I feel like I have maxed out the benefits of having it at my current position."

I had to repeat to myself "Its only lunch, its only lunch, you are married Nikki. He is your brother in law, Nikki. Nikki you are stupid, Nikki you are crazy." When I looked in the mirror my mind said to me "Nikki you are sexy, you sacrificed enough, do something for you."

I decided to tone it down, put my hair in a ponytail and opt for a pantsuit. I threw on some gloss, no lipstick because I was not going to let my sick obsession win. Jeff loved his plain ass wife. In that moment, I hated her. Jerome told me that she committed to this "plain Jane" lifestyle after the rotten things she did in grad school. She said if God forgave her she would be a picture perfect wife. If she can get forgiven, so can I. I put on my red lipstick, slipped on an A-line skirt and sped off in my BMW to see how I can "help." Jeff.

When I walked into Clydes, I instantly spotted Jeff sitting in the booth. In front of him sat a snifter of brandy and across from him I spotted a glass of red wine. The wine seemed to match his tie. When he spotted me he stood up, gave me a hug and a kiss on the cheek. He gestured for me to slide into the booth across from him.

"I ordered Malbec for you if you don't mind. Feel free to order something else if you like."

Damn, he ordered my favorite wine and he is wearing a tie to match! Damn!

"I love Malbec." I said, trying to contain my goofy schoolgirl excitement that one gets when the boy crush does something thoughtful.

"I am glad I can do something right." He placed his head in his hands

"If I do not do things according to Grace's project plan, regardless if she has shared it with me or not, I am automatically a loser."

I burst out into uncontrollable laughter. "A project plan?" I said through my laughter. "She is such a loser, who has time for a project plan, at home?" I was laughing so hard.

He lifted his head up and looked at me. He paused. I just knew I had offended him by calling his wife a loser and laughing in front of a full glass of Malbec. I could not even blame it on being drunk.

He broke his pause, and burst into laughter.

"She is just like her brother. Everything has to be status quo and everyone needs to just fall in line. Well honestly, I have fallen in line and out of love." Wait did I just say that?

Jeff's eyes widened. "Wait, you have fallen out of love?"

I felt like a fool, I am sure that I turned beet red. "Well, uh, um. Life is just so mundane. I wanted a little more passion. Some variety and little bit of risk...we are so um-vanilla."

"At least there is some flavor." Jeff said in a serious tone.

"Okay, back to why I need you." He sighed and pushed the statement of work across the table as I reached for the paper but somehow I grabbed his hand. Two hours and a bottle of Malbec later, in the backseat of my BMW I grabbed a lot more than his hands. I always felt so uncomfortable around Jeff but when he said "we can stop." I felt comfortable enough to say "I am tired of the status quo, aren't you?"

I sat at my steering wheel blaming Grace for my mistake. The meandering thoughts of justification for me luring Jeff into the back of my BMW with my unhappiness, my boredom, lust and my master's degree. UH! Grace is not squeaky clean! The only thing that is squeaking is her sins! I am not going to beat myself up over Mrs. Mediocre.

I drove home blinded by tears. What felt so good forty minutes ago now felt so dirty. After we were finished Jeff said "Thank you." He kissed me on the forehead and walked briskly to his car. He did not look back but it seemed like an eternity as I watched him walk away.

As I walked in the door, I almost tripped and broke my neck on a baby blue box. As I bent down and picked it up it was the unmistakable Tiffany blue. Before I opened the box a trail of rose petals led to the kitchen. There were pictures of me posted all over the room: my first communion, my high school graduation photo, 6th grade class photo. There was a sign above the staircase that says all the things to love about Nikki. On each baluster there was an index card. He index card said "I love Nikki because she is beautiful. I love Nikki because she is determined. I love Nikki because she is sexy." My mind said "I hate Nikki because she is a temptress." I instantly felt nauseous. My head started pounding and I ran up the Nikki tribute stairs. I ran into the bathroom and turned the shower on full blast. I heard the heavy thumps of Jerome's feet trudging up the stairs. "Nikki, what do you think?" He yelled. He sounded so proud of himself.

The hot shower beat against my skin so hard I thought it was going to peel off. All these years of being predictable and this fool decides to surprise me on the day I sleep with his brother in law in the backseat of my BMW. This shower is too damn hot! I am burping Malbec scented burps and I am just sick! I pounded the shower wall as Jerome desperately called out "Nikki, how do you like it?"

I woke up at 4 a.m. in my bed, wrapped in a towel. Jerome's arms were around me. I was so angry with him. I was angry with him for the guilt that I felt. I slid out of bed and ran down the stairs. I opened the tiffany blue box. It was a charm bracelet with a diamond infinity charm. I looked down and there was card. I opened it to Jerome's chicken scratch. Nikki I am sorry for losing focus on what's important "us." A month ago we had the most amazing sex. It started on the counter to kitchen floor and all the places in between until we made it to the bedroom. The kind of uninhibited sex that only married people can have. The next day I was cooking dinner and we would not eat it, because he said he that I did not properly disinfect the counter. The kitchen was contaminated and I should properly disinfect it before cooking in it at the day after a wild sex session. Jerome really knew how to really neutralize any spice that we had in our life. Now, the day I create a mess, he wants to focus on "us." This is a sick joke. I am nauseous again. I opened my bag to check my text messages; there is a text from Jeff "I asked God for forgiveness, I will never make the same mistake again." My heart pounded fast, I leaned against the wall and began my wall slide to the floor. Jeff managed to have to have adulterous sex with me and to get forgiveness within the same 24 hour period. Tears streamed down my dirty face. My stomach turned. Jerome finally had focus, Jeff had forgiveness and I had emptiness.

***

### Finding Grace

We were supposed to go Christmas shopping to take advantage of the Black Friday sales. Jeff's mom was going to watch the boys. At 7:00 a.m., she called wondering where we were.
I told her what a dog her son was. I told her that he was fucking that bitch. His mom seemed upset, but not at all surprised. She was sorry and she did her best to console me, but when we hung up, I wanted the world to know what a dog he was, how wrongly he had treated me.

I called his friends with whom he played tennis and asked if he was staying there because he was screwing my sister in law. I called his co-workers and told them to make sure he wasn't screwing their wives also. I called Jerome and did not get an answer. I called everyone I knew he knew and left messages that he was an untrustworthy excuse for a man, and they should not trust him at all or ever.

Nick was awake and wanted to make pancakes. He asked why Daddy was not there, and I told him that Daddy needed to leave for a while. He began to cry and ask why Daddy did not say good-bye. I called Jeff's cell and let him hear the tears of his son because he couldn't keep his dick in his pants.

Nikki had gotten to Jerome first. She gave him some song and dance about how it was a mistake and she was sorry and that they could work it out. And his dumb ass fell for it. I wanted to vilify her the same way I had Jeff - call all her friends and tell them what a slut she was. The problem was I had not let myself get close enough to her to disgrace her. I so wanted to disgrace her.

I took the boys to a childcare place even though Jeff offered to stay with them. I was not going to let him be alone with my children. It did not matter that they were crying to see him; whining to be with him; begging for me to let him in the house as he rang the doorbell repeatedly. He had not only cheated on me but he had cheated on them. He had debased the benefit of being their father by defiling their mother.

I went to see Sarah. I did not know who else to see. I cried and told her the story. She gave me vodka-a lot of vodka. I just didn't know what happened. Sure, we had our problems, but how did this happen? Sure he had affairs before, but this had a different feel. He had not even tried to explain about Nikki. He had not tried to make excuses to me. Was he thinking of leaving me for her? What did he plan to say to Jerome?

Sarah listened to my rant. After I finished, she assured me Jeff would not leave. When I asked how she knew, she simply said, "It is not God's will". She told me I would have to find a way to forgive them, but it was too early for that. For now, she just gave me a safe place to cry and try and heal my heart. She would be my angel while I learned to not demean Jeff in front on Nick and Jason. She would help me not be full of hate toward Jeff, Nikki and even Jerome.

I did not want to admit to my anger with Jerome, but if he had not been running off and chasing this dream of this business in California and had attended to his wife, then perhaps she would not have had time to be screwing my husband.

It was at Nikki that I was the angriest. I half expected Jeff to disappoint me. I expected Jerome to be as selfish as he had always been. But surely Nikki had had her heart broken in the past by some boy she thought was perfect. That boy or man may have even been my brother. So why would she inflict that same pain on another woman? Nikki and I had never been close. Okay, fine, I never liked her; but my expectations of her were much higher than that of the men in my life. In truth, I expected more from her because she was a woman not because she was or was not my friend.

Jerome did not divorce Nikki. They packed up and moved to California. Good riddance to the both of them. If Jerome was crazy enough to choose that tramp over his sister, then I hoped she would screw him over again. Perhaps the idiot would finally learn that she was worth less than zero.

Nick's and Jason's tears and pleas finally broke me. I allowed Jeff back into the house. He had agreed to counseling about his infidelity. The truth is, I wanted him to come back. It was a challenge raising twin boys with no strong male influence in the home. I needed the heavy tenor of his voice to snap the boys in line. I needed his presence to show them that a father does not leave. I did not, however, allow him back into our bed. I was not prepared to allow him back into my room. I could not forgive him like before. Nikki was too close to being a replacement. I found myself thinking about what may have happened if he had met her first.

Sarah asked me to attend her women's Bible study with her. They were doing a six week series on "forgiveness" and she felt I would benefit by attending. I was not in the mood to forgive. I was actually happy with my hate and misery. I was content to make Jeff suffer until I felt better. I could be happy when I chose to torture him with my presence and sideways looks or simply ignore his existence. So many times he asked if we could talk, and I would take the boys and barricade them in my room with endless movies and junk food.

I did not much care about Jeff when Nick and Jason and I were alone having our caloric feast. I knew that he did leave the house when we were in the room. He just armed the house alarm, and it did not go off again until morning. For all I knew he was looking at photos of Nikki and jerking off. Once Nick asked if we could invite Daddy in to watch a movie. I told him that Daddy was busy and needed to have peace and quiet. During the night, Nick left the room and I found him the following morning in the bed next to Jeff.

It was then I decided to go for the forgiveness sessions with Sarah.

***

During the first session, the instructor asked if we felt we needed to forgive anyone for any wrong done to us. I raised my hand. I was a victim and I was broken, and the instructor said just that; we had been wronged and spiritually damaged by someone we loved and trusted.
Yes! Yes! I thought. I am a victim. I am lost and heartbroken. She told me that God can heal all of that.

I had grown up in church, so I knew what God could do. All my life I had been taught to follow God's word and laws and that Jesus is my savior when I fall. It was never a question of whether or not he could, but if he would do it when I needed Him to. Then the instructor asked if we felt we needed to be forgiven for any wrong we had done. Dan was the first name to pop into my head, but I never felt guilty about Dan. He had pursued me. He was the one who seduced me when I was young and vulnerable. Now, looking back, I wondered why I did not say no to him.

I did not have to allow myself to be the one he pursued. I was actually stronger than he was because I did not carry his insecurities and baggage. I was not trying to escape and I should have realized that his love was not love at all. Under the flash, and the cars, and the dinners, he was just playing a game. There was something in my core that knew it, but looking back, I realized I did not care.

That Friday was the first night I asked Jeff to join the boys and me for our movie night. We popped corn and made s'mores in the microwave. I let him watch because he needed to be forgiven the same way I needed to be forgiven. I did not know if our marriage would survive, but I realized I needed to take a step. He was my husband for better or worse. I did feel about as bad as I could, but I had done damage too.

I was not naïve enough to completely absolve Jeff; but I could not deny my contribution. I did not have to emasculate him about his job. I knew it was an area he was sensitive about and I deliberately hit him where I knew it would hurt him; but had that made it easy for him? Did he think I did not love him? Looking back I had not acted like it. He had not either, but that certainly did not excuse my behavior.

I was still not ready to allow Jeff into my bed, but for once I did feel some type of hope.
Jeff and I started counseling through our church. We had joined Sarah's church and I signed us up for the *Building a Stronger Marriage in Christ* sessions held every Saturday. It was an 8

week session where you learn that you need to call God into your marriage. I figured, what did we have to lose? The Bible study had helped me see how I needed to forgive Jeff. Maybe this course could help our marriage. Our marriage was not much of one, so I signed us up.

Jeff seemed reluctant to attend, but my argument had been that if we did not do something, the boys would think this was normal for marriage and neither of us wanted that. They offered childcare for the hour long session, so we took the twins with us. We were not interested in sharing this endeavor with his mother, and I had barely spoken to Jerome since he and Nikki moved to California.

The course was designed to help you save your marriage, if it was possible, by making your marriage a priority and opening the lines of communication. The instructor had us do an exercise where one person would speak and the other would have to interpret what that person said, using their own words.

When it was Jeff and my turn, he said, "I feel you will never forgive me."

I deviated from the rules when I asked, "Do you want me to forgive you?"

Rules broken, Jeff said, "More than anything."

When the instructor asked us to stay on course, I said, "I heard that you want me to forgive you."

On my turn, I said, "I love you, but you hurt me a lot. It was more than Nikki; it was every time you made me feel I was not good enough for you."

Jeff looked sad, and said, "You have been hurt by me and you felt I wanted more than you."

With that our turn was over. Our homework was to practice that form of communication each day of the week until our next meeting.

When we got home I did not feel up to practicing. Those few intimate words exchanged between us had been more that we'd had in over six years. I was not sure I was ready to be open with him. I was not sure I could trust him by being open with him. It felt strange to realize how hesitant I was to be naked in front of my husband - not physically naked but emotionally naked. I had never told him about Dan and I never told him that I knew each time about his affairs. I was afraid to let him love me. The only time he had seen any glimpse of me was when I lost the baby. I needed to deal with that alone but without abandonment. Jeff had only done the later.

I prayed for strength and guidance before falling asleep. The next morning we fell back into our routine. We attended church followed by brunch and we went home and began our various chores to prepare for our week. We did not use our new communication tool at all that day.

The next day, Jeff called me at work and asked if I wanted to meet him for happy hour after work.

"Like a date?" I asked.

He laughed. His laugh was as sexy as I had remembered. He replied, "Yes. That is allowed, isn't it?"

I laughingly agreed and found myself anxious to meet him. We met at a quiet space of a local restaurant. I ordered a white wine and Jeff had a Jack with ginger ale. Jeff asked what I thought of our marriage session on Saturday. I felt my heart leap into my throat, certain he did not want to continue. He wanted to bail out. So I simply said, "It was fine."

"Fine is not the word I would use."

"What word would you use?"

"I would say it was enlightening."

That was the last thing I expected to hear from Jeff. He said he realized how much he never told me. He realized he was supposed to talk to me and that I should and could be his friend not just some woman he called "wife". He admitted he did not realize he was treating me like an object rather than a person and that he wanted to start anew.

I reworded what he said, using the new tool, and when he smiled, my heart melted as it had when we first started dating.

"I am afraid to trust you," I confided.

He told me that he felt that he needed to earn my trust. "All I want now is for you to let me try."

We picked up the boys from his mother who seemed happy to see us together. She offered to have Nick and Jason stay with her for the night, but we declined and stayed in our separate rooms again that evening.

Funny enough, our following session was about trust with communication. One spouse would put on a blindfold and the other would have to help navigate him or her through an obstacle course, using verbal commutation only. The problem was there were two other couples trying to do the same with their spouses. You had to focus on your spouse's voice and trust they were giving you the best path. You could not simply tell them, "Step over the box." You had say things like, "Raise your right leg and put your foot forward, then down." Jeff was blindfolded as I tried to navigate him through a tunnel, over a small wall and through different sized tires. He fell twice, but he laughed about it and said we would keep working on it. The next week, it was my turn to be in the blindfold. Jeff kept me out of harm's way, and I had to hug him, once I realized he had successfully talked me through a small maze complete with low hanging bars.

The sessions went on. Some were physical exercises and others were emotional. Other couples had shared their plights with infidelity. Even the instructors shared their issues with substance abuse and cheating on both sides, but God had healed them and then their marriages.

At the end of our eight weeks, we said our vows to each other again and Jeff and I celebrated by checking into the downtown Wyndham and having our "honeymoon".

"I promise, I will be a husband to you this time. I will take care of you. I want to be your Jabez."

I silently thanked God and drifted to sleep.

The phone rang late or early, I was too groggy to notice the time.

Jeff answered, "Hello. Yes. Jerome? Yes. What?

"Yes Jeff, Nikki is pregnant! "We are at LA General Hospital. I had to tell you. Before we moved to California, I wanted to do my sister a favor. I wanted to make her a widow by killing you slowly and watching you bleed out. I knew I was NOT giving up my beautiful, intelligent wife, so I decided it would not be fair to leave Grace without a husband. I did, however think of people in my network who would be a good replacement for your selfish ass. You know how Grace and I like to have a plan." Jerome sounded delirious. Jeff was not sure if it was due to lack of sleep or if Jerome was just overjoyed.

Jeff was instantly nervous. His mind flashed back to that afternoon. He knew that they used protection, but he could not help but be nervous. Then the shadow of guilt overcame him as he remembered how when he went to get gas before meeting Nikki at Clyde's that day and asking the cashier for condoms. He remembered how his mind plotted out a plan to have her and how it the moment manifested itself just as he planned. Now the guilt turned his stomach.

"Jeff! Snap out of it and calm the hell down. The baby is not yours, so stop shaking in your boots." Nikki has been pregnant for four months and had no clue. Today we spent the day in the ER, she had a fever. She had been working so much and we just assumed she was dehydrated. They could not get the fever down and she got really scared. She told me she had done the unthinkable and she needed to confess. The doctor came in with the results of her blood work and stated high HCG levels. He asked if he could perform and ultrasound. And there it was, our baby. I remember the day like it was yesterday, Jeff. That baby was made on the kitchen counter!! I told Nikki to confess to God not to me. We have made our mistakes. We all have things that we hide behind, things that we are not proud of. We all have things we cover. But God sees. If we repent he will show us his forgiveness. Our forgiveness is our baby girl. This is our chance to right all of our wrongs. Nikki almost pulled the IV out her arms. She has been shouting like crazy saying "Thank you God for hearing my prayers in spite of me! Jeff even in Nikki's stomach the baby looks just like me!"

Jerome's excitement was piercing through the phone. I heard every word that he told Jeff. I forgave Jeff, I forgave Nikki, but I never forgave Jerome for staying with Nikki. What was there to forgive him for? He did not do anything. He was a reserve for my anger. I could keep up the appearance of the forgiving wife who forgives her husband and his mistress, but I used Jerome as my arsenal of vexation.

There was a silent pause as the doctor came in to tell Jerome that Nikki's high fever has caused her to have a seizure.

***

I had not spoken to Jerome in over three months. I knew he left because he left voice mail messages to me. Even though I said I forgave Nikki, I wanted her to suffer by losing Jerome. I was upset with Jerome for reconciling with Nikki even though Jeff and I had. It seemed just too damn unrealistic for us to be the picture perfect family after our spouses had done the unthinkable. Now I would get the chance to tell him that I was sorry, he was hurting too and it was not his fault. I just always figured there would be time. Now Jerome could lose his wife and his baby, now is the time. I needed to be there for him. We were betrayed, but we are brother and sister and we promised mom and dad that we would stick together no matter what.

I could not feel anything at that point. I had not expected her to be pregnant. I was thankful that I could be confident that it was not Jeff's baby.

"I told Jerome that we would come."

I jumped out of bed and grabbed my iPad.

I will go. The boys have school. You have that presentation tomorrow, and you can meet me there after you get things squared away here. Four hours later, I was on the 8:24 a.m. flight out of Dulles to LAX.

As soon as I got off the plane, I ran into the hospital. Once I was directed to Nikki's room, Jerome spotted me and walked outside her room. I looked at my brother. He was exhausted. "Jerome, I got all of your messages. You moved here to make it easier for everyone. I wasted so much time wondering why you did not leave Nikki. There was so much time spent being angry at you for staying with her, while I rebuilt my life with Jeff. I wanted represent myself as snow white, a victim. It was not fair. Mommy and Daddy made it work. And we were doing what we were taught to do best, little brother, make things work. We do not have to be recognized by our faults, we have made our mistakes, we can use them to paint the best picture of ourselves and use them as lessons." He smiled and hugged me. I broke the embrace. "I am going to go in with Nikki. Go clean yourself up and get something to eat." I said.

She was still beautiful. How does she have several seizures, and still be beautiful? She looks beautiful and I look haggard. I have not had any sleep, nor coffee or a shower for that matter. I wanted her to live. I wanted her baby to live. I just wanted everyone to be normal again. I wanted to be the picture perfect family that everyone has come to know us to be. I sat quietly for some time before she opened her eyes and saw me.

"Grace?" Her voice was dry.

"Yes."

"You are the last person I expected." She was crying. "I'm so sorry," she said tears streaming down her face. "I never meant for anyone to be hurt. I know you hated me, but I never wanted to hurt you."

"It was easy to blame you," I told her. "But Jeff and I have never been closer. In a weird way, I have you to thank for that. We are open and honest, and he has been amazing to me. A better husband than he was before."

She smiled and coughed. "I had been praying. Jerome and I had been attending church here and I learned to ask God before I move. Wish I would have done that years ago," she mused. "I am worried about my baby; I have no other family. I asked God 'Please give my daughter a safe and happy home and a loving family' and here you are?" She asked it like a question.

And I looked at her like a question. Nikki was having a baby girl. I had lost a baby girl. Was this how it was supposed to happen?

"I forgive you," I told her. "I think if I would have been less jealous, we maybe could have been friends, and I think I would have liked that."

"I think I would have liked that too. Maybe you can show my daughter how not to be like either of us."

I kissed her forehead, I thought about how amazing God is. I am still hurt, my heart still remembers everything. But we all decided to move forward.

The doctor came in. "Your fever has downgraded, and the seizures have not affected the baby. Once you are stable you should be able to deliver a healthy baby girl.

"I am going to be a mother! Nikki cried aloud. "God, I said if you gave me another chance I would be a better wife, a better me. Little did I know, I had what I needed the whole time! Thank you!"

***

Life had come in full circle. As we embark on this new evolution, we know that we will not be making it alone. Being unfaithful destroys trust, it causes pain, and it builds walls. It seems impossible to move past infidelity, it seems impossible to rebuild when trust has been broken. The lesson of hurt makes one want to break free from what caused it. We can move forward with forgiveness despite the mistakes that seem beyond clemency. It is easy to say what mistakes are unforgivable until reality shows up at our door. Then there is the moment when we heal; when we show mercy and decide how to proceed from there. The beautiful canvas that we present to the world is painted by the mess that has become our message.

# VALUE
## Elevate –by Wendashia Ray

"He delivereth me from mine enemies: yea, thou liftest me up above those that rise up against me: thou hast delivered me from the violent man. (Psalm 18:48, KJV)"

*He walked into the T-Mobile store. She was working at the counter doing her beloved job, having the right to exist on her own terms. He poured gasoline on her, lit a match and threw it at her..he ran as she burned.*

I greet you as a brave, afraid woman, one who pushed past the obvious obstacles which could have kept my story in the coffins of so many who were tired enough to fight and those too scared to leave. I am walking past fear, embracing the 4,000 women per year who lose the battle to someone who has a broken mind and begins to physically and mentally break the woman he loves, his passion transformed, often times, into violence and obsession.

## A Ribbon in the Sky

We can't lose with God on our side
We'll find strength in each tear we cry
From now on it will be you and I.
And our Ribbon in the sky
Ribbon in the sky
A ribbon in the sky for our love
(Stevie Wonder, *Ribbon in the Sky*)

I was his best creation. He wanted me to be the greatest. His dream was to own a Cadillac, but his most prized collection was each sleeve that held the best vinyl records ever spun. My father had tons of records but this one I will remember forever. "You always remember what your grandmother told you. You are a Genius; I am your Daddy, and if anyone tries to mess with you, you come to ME." God gave you to me, and your Daddy will always be here for you, and when I get my Cadillac, you can sit in the front seat, and we will drive around the country. We will drive around to all of the colleges that you can decide to go to because you are going to be an engineer!

"Daddy, thank you for letting me be an engineer. I am going to be near engines? That is what an engineer does - stand near engines? Or do we make engines and then stand near them? Daddy, I can make the engine for your Cadillac."

Daddy laughed at me. A laughing giant, he was so tall, and as he laughed, he said, "You can make anything you want, but you need to go to college first. But, my little genius, you need to make it past your kindergarten graduation, and in order to get ready to graduate from kindergarten, you need to get your rest. Time for bed so you can get ready to learn your ABC's and 123's in the morning."

"I'm not tired, Daddy, and I am a genius and geniuses don't have a bedtime."

"Geniuses need sleep," Daddy said.

"I am NOT tired.

"Okay," he said. He flipped through the record sleeves and pulled out the one by my favorite singer-Stevie Wonder.

He held the record on the edges and places it on the spindle. The record started to spin and he dropped the needle. The piano started to play. Stevie Wonder began to serenade us with me and my daddy's favorite song: *Ribbon in the Sky*. Daddy grabbed my hand and told me to step onto his feet. I stepped onto his huge feet, my right foot on his left foot and my left foot on his right foot. I wrapped my arms around him and we began to dance. His feet moved left to right, and around in a circle. My eyes closed as another genius day came to an end. My father danced me to sleep. My daddy would never leave me, I did not even have to dance for myself; he danced for me.

> Oh so long for this night I prayed
> That a star would send you my way
> To share with me this special day
> where a ribbon's in the sky for our love.
> (Stevie Wonder, *Ribbon in the Sky*)

*\*\*\**

The doorbell woke me the next morning. It startled me awake until I heard my father talking to someone. Then I saw her at front door. She was beautiful, so beautiful, and there she stood, facing a gun that my father held straight at her. I thought only bad guys got shot not beautiful ladies like her. She seemed nice.

My father said "Get out of here!

I did not want her to get shot. I yelled at her, "Get out of here, Lady!"

She left. I was seven, and I saved her life.

"Pack your pajamas; we are going to Joyce's house."

I was convinced Joyce was a witch and she was going to lock me and my daddy in a cage. She looked older than my grandma. Everyone looked older than grandma. Everyone else's grandmas had wrinkly faces. I always wondered: where are my grandma's wrinkles on her face? I'm going to ask grandma if she is really a grandma. If she really is, I will tell her to ask the other grandmas how to get some of those grandma wrinkles.

Joyce had wrinkles. Maybe she wanted to be a grandma for my daddy. I packed my pajamas and my pretty pink dress that my grandma made for me. Joyce's little witch daughter may take my dress when I get locked in the cage. I grabbed my daddy's favorite record. We drove to Joyce's house.

It seemed like we were there forever. Joyce's daughters made me eat raw potatoes. I just wanted to spend time with my daddy; I had no interest in sharing my daddy with Joyce and her daughters any longer.

Then the day came that I found my father on the floor sick and vomiting. "Did she give you the nasty witch food, Daddy? Did she poison you?" He threw up and threw up and could not move. I called my grandma and she called 911, we would be leaving in an ambulance. I said, "Come on, Daddy, get up." I put the record on the record player. Come on, Daddy, get up. I'm going to stand on your feet, and we are going to dance." He didn't move....

The phone rang, and my grandmother whispered. She hung up, and she came and woke me up. She had tears in her eyes. I told her, "Don't cry, Grandma. He is a ribbon in the sky...and he is looking down on us from heaven."

Grandma lifted me up over the coffin. He was in his military uniform. Why did they dress him up for work if he was going to heaven? We were in a rest home. Each coffin had its own room, for the lifeless to corpses lay in expectation, for a visitor. It was so cruel. Everyone was on private display, dead yet expecting someone to come and show their respects. Pay respects to what? Death was the thing that took daddies away from 7-year-old little girls. I only saw the top half of his body. The bottom half of the casket covered the lower half of his body.

She lifted me above the coffin. For the first time I towered over my tall father as my feet dangled in the air. I looked at the lower half of the coffin and I said, "I cannot see his feet. This is not my daddy. I want to leave."

The guns shot in the sky, and they folded up the flag and put it in my hands. I looked up at the sunny sky and saw the smoke form ribbons and sneak towards the clouds.

My father was a Vietnam War hero who was now planted in a pine box among the daisies and beyond the headstones piled high upon dreams undone and unaccomplished. For some reason as we buried my father, in that sad moment, I wanted to dance. I wanted to have fun. I wanted to smile. Seven years old and I said good-bye to the man who would give his life for me to be the best me I could be, and he would never see me fulfill his dream. Yet I smiled. I wanted to dance.

At Grandma's house everyone was eating and sad. I ran around, and I danced. I laughed. I told my uncle Teddy that I wanted to put on a show. I handed him my daddy's record and said, "Put this on the record player. I am going to stand on your feet and we will dance. Let Grandma stand on your feet, Uncle Teddy. It will stop her from crying, and she will go to sleep. My daddy showed me."

"Sit down. No! We cannot have a show. This is a sad time!"

I went out to the porch with my record in hand, and a man rode down the street on his bike. He looked just like my daddy. I ran to the corner and as he stopped to wait for the cars to pass, I said, "Hey, hey, my daddy is in heaven."My record dropped to the ground. I looked at the ground and I looked up at him. I picked up my record. I held it out to him.

He said, "I am sorry your daddy is in heaven," and shook his head.

I tried to hand him the record.

He said, "You need to go home, and you should not talk to strangers, and I am a stranger."

Despite his words, I tried to shove the record into his hands.

He said, "I am sorry your daddy is in heaven." Then he sped off on his bike.        With my record in hand I ran, I ran, I ran, I ran. I shouted. I cried. I screamed! "Can I dance on your feet?"

My grandmother's eyes were full of tears as she kissed me and told me, "Baby, your daddy did not come here to stay and you did not either. The difference is, your Daddy is now in heaven and you should go back to your mother."

She packed my suitcase with my pretty pink dress. The witch's brats did not get my dress after all. "What I want you to understand is that you are a genius, and don't you ever forget that, so if I ever ask you a question, you don't get the right to tell me, 'I don't know.' You need to go and find out and give me the answer. Geniuses don't get to 'not know'." On top of my clothes she packed several books, and on top she placed the book, *I Know Why the Caged Bird Sings* by Maya Angelou.

My beautiful mother, the one I saw standing at the door as my father held a gun to her face. The one I told to "get out." She was now going to be the one to take care of me and bring me to a whole new life on the east coast. I smiled at my grandma and wiped her tears. I told her, "I know you miss my dad but I will always be your little genius."

Wow was I sorry for calling her names. Living with money was not half bad. I walked into a room fit for a princess - a bed with a canopy with a toy chest and dresses galore! And a record player with the needle placed on top of my favorite Michael Jackson song "Pretty Young Thang."

On my first day at my new school Sister Patricia introduced me to the class and escorted me to my seat. I told her that my grandma told me every day that I was a genius, and that she was lucky to have a genius in her class. Maybe the news would come and interview her for having a genius in her class. I told her because of ME she would be the famous teacher who got the chance to teach a genius.

I opened the book to see my father haunting my mind... lying on the floor, spitting up blood, just like the night he died. I opened my brand new book just to find myself there again; staring and the blood come from his mouth, his nose. Each heave took more and more life from him. Yet, I stood there still, lifeless, helpless, but a genius just the same.

I snapped back to the present to realize that I peed on myself at my desk. When I stood I slid and fell in the puddle. Walking to the office, I was a beautiful princess, covered in urine.

## Sister Act

I spent my elementary school years trying to get adjusted to my new life on the east coast. I missed my father. Life was speeding by so fast without giving me the happiness and acceptance that I felt with my daddy. I was excited for my 6th Grade year at my new catholic school Maria de los Santos. I walked into the classroom. Sister Clare told the class in her deep voice, very deep; the type of deep with made you wonder who was really under the nun's habit, "This is Zara. She's our new student." Everyone smiled. The blonde girl with a big red pimple on her forehead and bright metal braces on her teeth was smiling at me and so was the boy with the freckles. Everyone was smiling at me. Yes I was the star of the show and those smiles were saying, *Hey be my friend!!* They must have liked me because all of the students in the school were white. *Yay, they are so happy they finally got a black person to go to their school.*

"NIGGER," the boy with the freckles said to me as I sat in my seat and opened my desk.

Well, that certainly was not *Hey, be my friend.*

I said, "No, no, you said the wrong thing to me. The name is Zara."

"No, the name is Nigger, N-I-G-G-E-R."

All the other smiling kids snickered and laughed

People pay all this money to Catholic schools, and this is all they learn how to spell?

Sister Clare began writing on the chalkboard and said, "When you get to high school, you will see problems like this: $5(x-6)-3(x-7)$. Given what you know now, what could you do to simplify this?"

Michael, the boy with the freckles, was called to stand at the board. He had no idea how to simplify the problem. His face turned so red that his freckles almost disappeared.

I raised my hand and went to the board and computed the entire problem. After I was done I said, "What is your name?"

He squinted at me with his fire red face and said nothing.

I said, "It seems that you have been working on your spelling and not your math. Sister Clare was wrong. You do not have to get to high school to do math like this. I have been doing this since last year. But since you like spelling spell this: G-E-N-I-U-S. That's me. Nigger is an ignorant person, and since you cannot do this eeeeeasy math, and I can, that makes you the NIGGER--NOW SPELL IT!" I wanted to slam his pretty round red face into the math problems on the chalkboard. Maybe that would help him comprehend.

Tears streamed down his face. Sister Clare sent me to do penance. I was to kneel with my rosary and recite 20 Hail Marys. "Hail Mary Full of Grace," I was glad to spend my time with Mary. I was safe with her and my rosary. "Hail Mary full of GRACE."

\*\*\*

Those memories all come to mind as I find myself at my moment of truth. I am finally ready to tell a 21-year-old nightmare, one I didn't hear much about until it publicly affected athletes and celebrities. Before it became the priority of the NFL, I was tackled by this 21 years ago and it completely gave fear a permanent residence within my life. I thought I was ready to take this on - me, miss brave writer, but now I am afraid, afraid to tell this story. I am going to tell this story afraid. As my pen gets tortured through this agony I feel that I am still going to press through it. I may be afraid now, but then I was terrified. So, for my condition to be upgraded to afraid, you can now put away that freshly pressed and bleached straight jacket and send the doctors home to rest. Let me give myself some credit. As terrified as I was, I was brave. I was smart. I was the dumbest smart girl I know.

I told a friend one day that I was volunteering with women affected by domestic violence, and she said, "Why, what do you know about domestic violence? You have never been affected by domestic violence."

Yeah, that's what the police told me. This is the reason I lived with the nightmare for three years---three years, wide awake in a nightmare of people convincing themselves I was not abused. My mind sinks back to the moment as if it was yesterday.

I was thirteen years old; heading from a catholic school in Truedale to another school-- Woodbridge, a private school for girls. Only the brightest, most talented girls got into Woodbridge. I was the elite; I was awesome. I went from Catholic school girl to college preparatory girl. "No one is worthy of speaking to me because I am too perfect. I am smart, I am talented, and nothing you can say can make it to my level."

This led me to my first fight. I was smart and I was the toughest girl on the block. So after I got my ass beaten, I still had my intelligence.

My mother was strict. I spent every evening after school babysitting because my mother worked two jobs and on the weekend her job was her boyfriend. Welcome to the life of Cinderella. Cinderella could not so much as talk to a boy. Her mother would not have it. But what do teenagers do best? Exactly what their parents do not want them to do.

I had one friend that my mom hated to have me even be around. When my mother was at work, it was my opportunity to be around her. Why did I have to be around Faith? Faith gave me access to all of the boys.

The boys loved Faith because her jeans were always tight and she was very generous with the use of her body. Let just say the boys "had a lot of Faith." When my mom as at work, and my grandmother would keep my siblings to relieve me from my nightly childcare shift, Faith and I would have the best parties. Grandma would be coming in the front door and the boys would be jumping out the back window. But the boys would be there to have a little "Faith". They paid me no attention except to thank me for allowing them into my house and letting them eat my snacks and take advantage of Faith's generosity.

I have always been the social butterfly, but a butterfly is beautiful. Let's just say I was the social moth. I was dark skinned with short hair. My mother had it processed so much that it all fell out, so I was blessed with a wet and shiny Jheri Curl. I didn't have many clothes, but the ones I had were really nice. The two things in my favor that made the boys want to come around me were: my house had a bar, and my mom worked nights. Oh how soon a moth becomes a butterfly.

The crazy thing is I made sure to do my homework first before the after school parties began. It was an afterschool special at best - teenagers drinking and smoking marijuana, and me the hostess with the most-est, sitting snug on the couch with her favorite drug: an algebra book. I had no interest in alcohol, or drugs, but I did have a keen interest in books and boys.

I was not interested enough to do the things that Faith would do. The boy's penises would find a home in her mouth. I would ask her, "Why do you let them put that in your mouth? Why don't you just show them to the bathroom? I have two bathrooms, Faith. You do not have to let them put that in your mouth"

She would laugh at me, and say, "The boys love you when you let them do that."

I liked the white boy named David. Since I was so dark, I wanted the complete opposite. We would play Nintendo and sneak tongue kisses. I felt free and loved. I felt as though I had one up on Faith because I could have the boy without the sex. Since Faith was light-skinned, I felt I had an advantage over the light-skinned girl. My mind would not let me think that the guys loved Faith because she would let them live out their fantasies with her body and especially her mouth. I felt they loved her because she was light-skinned.

So, yes, here is the girl with the issues - insecure, looking to boys for validation and always seeking a good time and companionship. Instead of daily after school parties I needed an after-school therapist and bible study. This went on for about a year. During that time I started to blossom. Because I ran a mile to the bus stop, I started to thin out. My mother found a hairstylist for me who thankfully decided to crucify the jheri curl. My mother invested in some new clothing for me. My new hairstylist showed me how to do hair and made me the shampoo girl so I could earn and thus get my new-found beauty for free. In feeling beautiful, I felt free.

**Back to how I met Mr. Broken**

Do you remember who you think was your first love and all the craziness you did to keep him? My craziness almost landed me in the peace of a coffin. Ahh, Ryan, my first love. "Well you know Ryan allows a nasty girl to live with them, and she is super nasty, and nasty with several people. You better get your bottom checked."

All of the sudden the chair I was sitting in became too hard. My bottom could no longer stand it, as my mind was clouded with the fear that it might not be the chair that was too hard, but the disease that was taking a hard toll on my bottom.

This is where life finds me on the bus to the clinic. I was in danger of possibly being tainted with the sins of someone that I did not even have the pleasure of sleeping with. Oh but Ryan was having a great time with his live-in lover, and I was his high school supplement. Yuck!!

"Oh honey you are free and clear!!" As I left with enough condoms to supply an all-boys high school, the nurse pleaded with me for me to protect myself. She almost bent down on one knee.

I rolled my eyes and said, " I did protect myself, but I was scared that what I may have contracted could burn right through a condom," Thank God the chair was too hard and my bottom was not on fire, but my life was about to be.

I had to find a way to make Ryan jealous. I wanted him to want me and not be able to have me. I needed to teach him a lesson that would school him enough to put miss nasty girl and her belongings out on the curb.

I called my friend Thomas. He was so cool. He spoke with a low voice, so low that you could not understand a word that he said. Since Thomas went to school with Ryan, he knew that Ryan had an ego bigger than homeroom. He knew that Ryan would not want everyone to know that his pretty little girlfriend with the hot body and pretty dark skin was now the property of his rival -Trevor. Yes, property. That's what we girls in Holland were - property. Only few accepted anything different. We strived to have a boyfriend, to be loved to be owned, for someone to say "You are mine." To get married, to have babies, to get a good job right in Holland. We were not encouraged to move around the country or internationally. Ryan's property was now being taken over by Trevor.

Thomas explained to me that Trevor and his girlfriend had just broken up, and Trevor, since he hated Ryan, would be a great short term way to make Ryan jealous.

In my mind I said, "Perfect. When Ryan gets jealous and begs for me to come back, I can drop this loser whose girlfriend gave him the boot."

The day I met Trevor, I walked up to him, saying to myself "This is only temporary, this is only temporary, this is only temporary, "the way we say it does not hurt when we burn our finger on the stove, yet we walk around blowing on it, saying, "It doesn't hurt."

He looked at me as if he just saw a celebrity. He said, "Wow, Thomas did not tell me that you were this beautiful."

My head spun as my mind journeyed to a place where my hands were wrapped around Thomas' neck because Trevor was not cute enough to make my dog jealous. I would be sure to make sure my dog bit the hell out of Thomas when I saw the sneaky bastard.

I was famished so he took me out for a sub at Luccino's. It does not matter where he took me. The point is, he viewed me as some sort of celebrity, some sort of prize. When we were in the long line at one of the most popular sandwich shops in the area with the line out the door, he constantly reminded me that the guys were checking me out.

I smiled and said to him, "Is there something you need to tell me? It seems like you are checking out the guys, and you are jealous because they are checking me out. Don't worry, sweetie," I said, "there are enough guys in here for the both of us."

He looked at me and said, "I cannot believe you are standing here with me with your smile, that body, your hair, your dark skin."

(Did he say something nice about my dark skin? That would be an upgrade from being called "charcoal". I might start to like this guy.) My mind rationalized, *He is not that bad. After all, he bought me food.*

"I can see why all the guys want you, but I am going to make you mine." Yeah, "make" was the right word. I told him I would be attending Woodbridge School.

He told me that his mother was a cook there.

I said "Good. I like her already."

When school started I did not realize how time consuming being smart was. My school expected me to be well rounded, encouraging me to dance and play field hockey, and that was only week one. Because I lived in a neighboring town thirty minutes away, Trevor would bring me home from school. His "girl" could not be on the bus. I would have gladly ridden the bus with Ryan. I missed him. One day when I got home from school there was a call from him. "Hey there Zara, look I miss you." He started to sing, "I will always love you, when you're lonely, I will..hold you."

I was hooked, a sucker for a song. Yes even the birds caught my eye when they sang a pretty tune.

"Look, Zara I heard that you are dating Trevor. I am not trying to act jealous, but I am. I am more so worried about your safety. He used to beat his ex-girlfriend. One time he beat her so badly that he knocked her out cold. He thought that she was dead. He put her in a plastic bag and put her in a dumpster. Luckily she woke up and clawed her way out of the bag."

My eyes widened. "Oh Ryan, that sounds crazy. I am sure that did not happen. He is so nice, but a loser just the same. Ryan, my dear, your apology is accepted. You do not have to make up horror stories about Trevor." I smiled and said "Let's make up over an ice cream cone at the mall, and if you sing to me you will make that ice cream much sweeter and I may just let you kiss me."

"Singing. Kissing. Ice Cream---YOU-YES!"

"One thing before we start singing, kissing and ice creaming: is the nasty girl still taking residence at your mother's house?"

"A month ago my cousin came over to get my baseball glove. When he took too long and I was late for practice, I came home to find out why he was so late. The nasty girl decided to give him her personal glove, around his penis. She saw me and ran out of my house naked. I stood at the door and just looked into space. I felt so stupid. My naked cousin went to the back room and grabbed my baseball glove. He handed it to me and said "You must have come back for this." He handed my glove to me and proceeded to get dressed."

"Maybe that's your lucky glove; it makes people get naked." Yes! My planned worked. I got my Ryan back. It's time to tell Trevor thanks but no thanks. After practice I made sure I kept on my smelly field hockey gear. I kept my hair in a ponytail and did not bother to wash the sweat off of my face. By the way I looked, I was sure Trevor would be dumping me. I would be sure to look broken hearted.

He pulled up in the car and I hopped in. He looked at me, and smiled and opened up a black box with a diamond ring with a gold band. Oh God, Oh God. I am 14 years old and this fool wants to marry me? He leans in and kisses my cheek and says, "I want you to be my love forever. Will you marry me?"

"Trevor, maybe the smell of my sweat has gone to your brain. I am not even old enough to drink and for me to marry you I would need to be very drunk. I am 14!" I looked at the band and it said 14kt. It was real. I looked at him. His feelings were real. I hated him for loving me. That was not part of the plan.

"Look, Trevor. I'll be honest. I asked Thomas to set us up to make my ex-boyfriend Ryan jealous. I was not looking for anything long term when I started seeing you. I know you love me and want me to be happy. You should be happy to know that Ryan is jealous and he wants me back, and I want him too." Then I smiled a big white smile.

And that was the day I took my first punch to the face - not a local schoolyard fight but a prizefighter punch to my face. As my head hit the window the only words I could find were, "What did I do?"

His jaw hardened, and his eyes turned red, a monster in a horror movie yet human enough to put his hand on my head and begin to bang my head against the seat. My head started to ache. I was dizzy. I vomited.

He stopped and stared at me and said, "Clean it up."

I went to open the door to run. Then the words I would learn to hear day after day came out of his mouth. "Bitch I will kill you."

I took off my jersey and started to wipe the vomit from his leather car seats. Trevor drove me home and apologized over and over again, and then to add insult to injury, his tears began to flow. REALLY, he is crying? How does this work? I am the punching bag, but he gets to cry? What stars align to create this backward scenario? As he cried, sniffed and snorted I looked out the window and prayed that he would drive faster and shut up.

We got a block away from my home, and before I got out of that car he asked: "Please don't leave me. Just give me a little more time. Please. If you leave me, I will kill myself. Please. Please don't leave me.

I thought to myself, "Great. I will have a death on my hands." I slammed the door, and as I walked down the block to my house, my heart began to turn to stone.

As I opened the door my mother shouted, "Are you ready for dinner?"

"No, I am tired from the game and I have homework." I ran up the stairs, ran into the bathroom and turned on the shower. If there was a setting that was "Ice cold", that was the one that the shower was turned to. I let the cold water splash my face and cool my head. I slid down the shower wall and sat on the shower floor. I let the cold water cool go where his punch landed and cool my throbbing head. As the cold water danced on my head I felt the warmth of hell.

The next morning as I headed to school, my face was sore but I did not have any bruises. In my morning prayer I said, "God please make Trevor disappear." When my mom was driving me to school I looked in the side mirror to see Trevor's car five cars behind us. Then I looked to the sky and in my mind I said, "God you do not follow directions well at all. I asked you to make Trevor disappear, not show up 5 cars behind me." I would have to deal with God later. For the moment I had to turn my attention to how to get rid of this freak.

My day was full of Spanish and math quizzes that I managed to fail. My Spanish teacher said, "Que pasa, mi hija." She wanted to know what happened and I did too. I had never seen an F in my life and she had the nerve to write it in red. I told her it would never happen again.

As I walked out of school, he was waiting there. I walked to the car and he said please get in. I just want to talk. I got in and he lifted his hand. I froze as I felt the urine flow down my leg. I started shaking and screaming.

"Pleassssssseeeeeee!"he said in a half whisper, "I promise, I promise, I will never do that again. I don't know what happened. I am so sorry. I promise I will never do that again."

In that moment I thought, *I am 14 years old, and I peed on myself.* He drove me to his house and opened the door for me to take a shower. He was gone for about an hour and a half and returned with a Victoria's Secret bag and a bag from the Calvin Klein store. I slid into my new garments. It was amazing how new clothes can make a person feel human again. The kicker is, *IT'S ONLY TEMPORARY.*

Then there it was again, the black felt box accompanied by another two long boxes. One was a diamond bracelet, the other a gold necklace with a diamond charm. "Please just wear these. Just stay with me and try to forget about Ryan. If in a month you still don't want to be with me, then I will let you go."

The vision of the calendar and my countdown had begun, 30 days. I literally saw the chains breaking and me running free, free from all men.

**Day one**:

In the lunchroom his mother saw my new gold and diamond bling and said "Oh you are supposed to be engaged now." She laughed so hard. Yet her laugh had a hint of pity, a hint of fear, but no hint of hope.

**Day two**:

After my game, he picked me up and watched me do my homework, I taught him three words in Spanish.

**Day three**:

Great conversation, and no word from Ryan, Trevor does not seem as bad.

**Day four**:

Trevor takes me on a shopping trip after school.

**Day five**:

Trevor picks me up from getting my new haircut.

**Day six**:

Trevor picks me up from school; I have my new haircut, and I have on my new clothes. I close the door and look at Trevor. His face looks like stone. I hear the crackle of the gravel as we turn into the alley. My heart begins beating fast, I want to run. I look at him and the corners of his eyes are red, I begin to cry for some reason. His silence tells a million stories of what is to come next. He grabs me by my head and pushes my face with his other hand. Then he starts hitting me in the face with no words.

I honestly cannot tell how long this lasted, but the part that hurt the most was my throat from my screams. No one was there, no one. Daddy, where are you now? You said you would never leave me. I guess I will have to take up this issue with you in heaven, as it looks like I may be joining you there soon.

Trevor whispered a question in my ear. "Who are you trying to look good for?"

I did not know how to answer this question, but I gave it my best shot and I said "Me."

Trevor resumed his one sided prize fight.

**Day seven**:

I walked out the back door of my school and began my journey to the bus stop home. Trevor zoomed up to the side of me and acted as if he was going to hit me with the car. I began to run and he speeded up. I could run but I just couldn't seem to scream. Trevor did not have the same problem. "Get in the car now!" He yelled.

I obeyed him because being ran over was not the way I wanted to die. He sped off, and we drove to his house. We walked into the room, and he paced and paced and paced. I was hoping he tripped over the mass amounts of clothing all over the place. He paced and paced. Then he said "I asked for 30 days."

I said, "Well, according to my calculation you started hitting me for no reason on day 6, and tried to hit me with your car on day 7, so we can safely say you ruined it, you fucking sicko"

I was certain if I just said something mean, he would put his tail between his legs and GO AWAY.

His face hardened.

I said, "If you are going to hit me again, it is getting old."

He dropped to his knees and began to cry and beg and say, "Please forgive me. I will do anything. Just please forgive me."

I looked at him on his knees. I lifted his face in my hands, balled my fist and started punching him with all the hate, anger, sadness, pain and loss I had.

He pushed me onto the ground and held me down with his foot. He reached behind himself and pulled out a gun.

I stood up and I looked at him.

"I will kill you, your mother, your brother and your sister. You deserve to die. You are crazy."

I frowned, I questioned in my mind how I was the one who was crazy, but I was not the one with a gun. He pulled the trigger and he fired the gun. When my brain realized I was still alive, I turned to him and said, "I forgive you."

**Day eight**:

I went to the police station after school. I asked to file a report. I told them that my boyfriend kept hitting me and he shot a gun. They asked for his address, and brought me there to show them where the gun was shot. I led them to the room and started to look for the bullet hole. I got on my knees and I scrambled through the clothes and scaled the walls. There was no bullet hole. The police did not believe me. I had no bruises, no bullet holes, just the knowledge that my day 30 freedom would never come. My reality was stuck on day 8, turned on its side, now an infinity.

# Hello from the Grave

At 14 years old and I felt like my life was cut short, yet I lived and breathed, smiled, yet cried and shook at night. I was to be the next Thurgood Marshall, protector of civil rights, a path right to a seat on the Supreme Court. Who the hell was protecting my civil rights? Who was protecting me when his big body was on top of me sweating, pressing, kissing ….GROSS!

Added to my disgust is the pain of a punch. "Who do you think of when you are with me? Are you thinking about him? Are you sleeping with him?" As my eye throbbed and began to swell, I looked around the room and asked, "Is there anyone in the room with us? My eye is swollen shut so I cannot see out of it and I am seeing double out of the other. So now it looks like there are two of you Trevor, but in reality there is just you, no one else in this room. So how can I be sleeping with you and someone else at the same time?"

"I assume that you are satisfied. I guess punching turns you on. Does it make you tingle inside, Trevor, punching women? Is it foreplay for you? They did not teach us in sex ed that punching was a form of foreplay. Can I punch you Trevor? Maybe it would make sleeping with you more enjoyable, because really, Trevor, it just sucks. Trevor, can I punch you?"

I was looking through one eye at a man of stone, even the shape of his face hardened as his hands formed fists and the punches came one after one. The thing about pain is it just stays there and says to you, "Do not complain. I am pain, and I do not go away. Learn to live with me. Learn to endure." The punches came, and the pain did not go away. It got stronger with each punch and with each punch I learned to live with it. I listened to pain. I endured.

I went home and explained to my mother that I took an elbow in the eye at practice.

***

Then the phone rang. I answered; he hung up. The phone rang. I answered; he hung up. The phone rang. I answered; he hung up. I broke the ringer on my mother's phone to make sure she did not answer. Trevor told me that if he ever called and she answered he would say to her: "You dumb bitch; that's why your boyfriend beats you."

Yes I was dumb enough to believe that if Mr. Broken knew that my mother's boyfriend beat her, he would stop beating me. I thought he would see the cycle. Yes, I wanted the guy who did not see the value of attending high school anymore, and put more effort into buying a souped-up new car, to be able to recognize a cycle and attempt to break it.

Unfortunately, I was dating an abusive high school drop-out, NOT a psychologist. The only cycles this maniac knew about were motorcycles and menstrual cycles, neither of which gave me a reprieve from his sexual obsession with me.

How could he think this was fun? Me, laying on my back staring at the ceiling, thinking about my next lacrosse game or my next AP history exam. As soon as I felt him stiffen I would wiggle away to force him out. He was always too heavy. He was physically heavy and a mental weight, an anchor pulling me right to the bottom of the ocean.

He was way too heavy and his little mini crazies were swimming their way to where my hopes and dreams awaited the husband of my dreams, not the crazy broken man of my nightmares, my reality.

When he finally rolled over, I ran to the bathroom and turned the water on scalding hot and full blast. I took the removable shower head put it between my legs and tried to obliterate the crazies he released inside of me. I knew if I became pregnant, it would drive a nail in the coffin I already call home.

My reddish-brown headstone would say: "Here lies the fool who wanted to make her boyfriend jealous, by dating a certifiable maniac. She was so smart, so strong, so brave."

It was Tuesday and my AP history paper is due the next day. What made Henry the VIII have his young wife hung? For some reason I loved Henry the VIII. I enjoyed learning about him. I loved hearing how his love affair had caused him to cause an entire religious revolution. I could not wait to take the test. I was so excited. Excitement in my life was only a luxury that would last in ten minute intervals. It is like Mr. Broken could smell that I was happy and he could not sleep until he sabotaged it. RING! RING! RING! RING! RING! RING! RING! RING! 51, 52, 53, 54, 55, 56 -DAMMIT why doesn't Verizon cut in on the line and say, "Fool, obviously they do not want to talk to you."

I thought Verizon should implement a limit on how much one person can call another without an answer. Verizon, please refuse this man phone service. I need to call a congressman to invent legislation to have phone privileges taken away from those who use the phone to harass someone to satisfy their sick obsession. Somehow I broke my mom's ringer so it would not ring, but when I tried to break mine, it did not work. If I took the phone off the hook and my aunt called and heard the busy signal, she would drive over to make sure we are okay. RING!!!! RING!! Oh hell, I would have to chance her driving over here because I needed to pass the AP test.

Mr. Broken had to take his aunt to the doctor that day, so I had a break. I stopped by the library on my way home and picked up a copy of the "Joy Luck Club". I hoped his aunt got diagnosed with something that required his 24 hour care. Then Trevor would have no time for me. Ah, misery made me wish a terminal illness on a completely innocent person just to free myself from what was slowly killing me.

I went home and made a peanut butter and jelly sandwich, and turned on the news. For some reason I needed background noise to enjoy my book because I was so used to the phone and it's incessant ringing.

"There was a shooting today at Shulster circle. There are three black male victims. We will be scrolling their names on the bottom on your screen if you have any information please contact, 216-712-8989." I got so excited. I could not wait to see his name scroll across the screen. . I would say "YES!" and start singing the "Freedom" song. He would finally be out of my life. This was AWESOME. Trevor lived on Shulster Circle."THERE WAS A GOD!!"

I screamed, "Oh, please, let this be my lucky day! Oh, please, let this be my lucky day!" I anticipated those names the way my mom anticipated her lottery number popping on the screen to say she hit the mega millions.

Drum roll..the names: "Samuel Edwards, Jose Morales, and Cortez Jesus." Clearly they were Latino. DUMB news can't even get the victims nationality right. I hope their families sue

News 12. I HATE them. I hate them because they could not do me a small little favor of giving me the joy of knowing he Trevor Richards was out of my life for good.

The stupid murderer or murderers were right in the neighborhood and they seemed to avoid the most damaged, broken, evil fool on the street, the one who needed to be put down like the rabid, mad dog that he was.

The ringing began. This fool would probably call me from the grave!

Once the ringing stopped, I finally fell asleep. I had a dream that was full of screams, broken glass, and crying. Yet I slept right through it. It was such a peaceful sleep not even tragedy could awaken me. When God finally nudged me to wake up, I realized I had overslept. My mother had not screamed my name to get me to school. When I opened my bedroom door I thought we had been robbed. The TV was on the ground and broken dishes and glasses were on the floor. I ran to my brother and sister's rooms and they were sound asleep. I chuckled to myself that they would sleep through anything as long as no one touched their toys. I felt sick to my stomach as I remembered the dream I'd had, and I ran to my mother's room. There she was, lying on her bed full of blood, and she looked just like the elephant man. Her face was swollen and disfigured. I opened the door and she asked me to hand her the phone. She wanted me to call him at work. She told me to ask him "Why."

I was scared of her, scared of the blood, and scared of "Why." I could not move my fingers or my lips. Finally I muttered out, "I need to call 911." Why call 911 when they did not seem to believe me when I told them I had been beaten by my boyfriend? For some reason I did not have enough bruises for the police to help me. I mean, hey, I lived in a town where a man shot his wife in a domestic dispute and drove her to the hospital, and somehow still walked around free as a bird. I was sure that the fact that my mother was looking like the elephant man was not enough to get them to respond. I assumed unless they needed to bring a body bag it was not priority. "Do not call 911. He said he was sorry, but I just want to know why, what made him do this."

I said, "He does it all the time. Will you knowing why make him stop?"

"I am fine," she said, "Once the swelling goes away, I will be just fine"

"Your face looks broken, not swollen. How do you fix a broken face? Maybe instead of asking why, you should ask how you are going to fix your broken face! I am not calling him, and if I do I would ask him to bring a broom to clean up all the stuff in the house that I have to clean. I would ask him to do all the school work that I am going to miss today and all the school work the kids are going to miss, and finally I would ask him to bring a surgeon to fix your broken face!"

"Get out! Get Out!"

"Yes I will get out and get you some ice and hopefully it works since you have deluded yourself to believe that your face is just swollen, when I know it is broken!. But hopefully as the ice melts your face will return to normal."

My sister and brother were still sound asleep. I guessed I'd have to miss a day of school icing down her face, while she tried to figure out why. This was the same town that was nationally known as the capitol of domestic abuse, and she wanted to know why.

I brought her a bucket of ice. "Just put your face in there and maybe it will return to normal, I went to my room to study for my AP calculus test. On my way to the room I looked out the window to see him waiting outside in the cul-de-sac in his shiny new red car. *Way to be inconspicuous, stalking your girlfriend in a red car. Well Trevor you will not get the chance to follow me and my mother from home to school in the morning…………*

*Dear Doll,*

*Your name is doll because I am just over the age to be playing with baby dolls. Yet I feel the tickle of your little feet kick me on the inside and your father's feet kick me on the outside.*

*They didn't believe me. They said, "You are an active teenager. Bruises happen all of the time. Where are the bullet holes from gun you claim he shot in the house to let you know he would kill you?"*

*I looked around the messy house, under clothes, everywhere. The only holes I found were in a worn out shirt. The round policeman, as we walked out the door, shook his head and said, "You children watch too much television and it is making you dream up some crazy things. You seem like a smart girl. Use that imagination to make something of yourself. "*

*Doll, I told the people with the signs who wanted me to give you a chance, that he was going to kill me. They told me that I should "take my chances on being killed in order to avoid being a killer."*

*He told me as soon as you arrive he will shoot you because he does not believe you are his. He said that he will kill us both before my due date. Yet I am the murderer. A 14-year-old murderer.*

*I think if I kill myself, I will do it kindly, not like the brutal, bloody, heinous way I will die at his hands. Doll, I will be good to us. I will take us out of here beautifully and peacefully - just to take the joy away from him, the excitement and joy and sense of accomplishment he would feel from beating me to death. He will not get that chance I will beat him to the punch.*

Hmmm, what in this house can kill me? I tore apart the medicine cabinet and all I could find was Tylenol. SHIT. Too bad no drug addicts lived in the house offering me the luxury of having access to something stronger. Tylenol? Damn! I wanted to kill myself, I didn't have a headache!

When I had cramps I could not get the damn bottle to open. I swore it was a strategy to make you yearn for Tylenol like crack when you had menstrual cramps. I swore it was what kept them in business. The cramps began to hurt so badly your mouth began to water to the point where you felt you were going to vomit, and then *pop* - that big bulge of cotton was sitting right on top for you to have to dig out with all your might. It was like they put reams and reams of cotton in there, and once you got to the bottom of it, popped open like a river raft, and then there they were... the dreamy pills that you poured down your throat praying that they killed the cramps right away.

Today, however, I needed them to kill another pain, and hopefully rid me and doll of the pain in my ass.

The label warned "do not take with alcohol" so I figured if I drank it with gin I would be on the midnight train to hell. I do not remember how many I took as I washed them down with gin. It was clear like water but it burned like the hell that I was sending myself to. I said, "Doll, here is where we part ways. You will go in one direction, and I will go in the other. Say hi to God for me and I'll brag on your behalf to the devil and say 'HA HA, you couldn't have her.' Doll, I saved you from the Devil."

I would rather go to hell then ever have to see Trevor again. He would probably follow me there. The thing about the devil, he would want me all to himself. He would not dare share me with Trevor. He would probably kick Trevor out of hell because hell with me eternally would be heaven for Trevor.

My grandmother really believed I was a genius. Even though I would smile when I was in pain (and she was a little concerned that I might be a little slow) she would smile her beautiful smile and say I was a genius. After the day I tried to ride her on her mini poodles back like he was a horse she hugged me tightly and said, "My little genius, you have such an imagination. Use that to do something great one day."

Well, Grandma, I am sure you saw your little genius from your seat in heaven as I woke up throwing up gin-scented vomit as doll's feet fluttered in my stomach. The "genius" could not even figure out a lethal enough formula to kill herself. So much for advanced placement chemistry. They could not even teach me how mix the right dose to bring me to eternal rest. That class was a waste of time. They needed to fire the teacher. He seemed a little distracted anyway.

I broke down and cried. I recited the bible verse my grandmother told me "I will lift my eyes to the hills, which cometh my help, my help comes from the Lord."

I had to look somewhere for help because it was not coming from the police.

I dressed myself for school so my mother could take me. I got in the car and put my seatbelt on. As my mother began to drive, she talked about how when I graduated she was going to dance all night because I would have accomplished her dream of graduating from one of the most prestigious schools in the United States. I looked at her, and I smiled as the ice had miraculously begun to heal her face.

Then I was struck by reality again as I looked in the side view mirror. I thanked God that my mom dreamed of me graduating and did not share the nightmare of my reality. The reality of the psychopath who made it his daily routine to follow us through town each and every morning with his window slightly cracked to remind me that he would easily place a gun through the window and kill my mother and then me.

It confused me how someone managed to keep control of a car while pointing a gun out of the window. It was a shame that Trevor did not use that coordination for something more rewarding in life. Since he had the discipline to get up early in the morning and drive to a school, why didn't he drive to his own school and get his diploma! He did not even deserve to look at my school. I chuckled as I imagined him going cross-eyed looking at my Advanced Placement Calculus book. He had told me if I alerted my mother that he was behind us, he would shoot us. He described how my mother's brains and mine would cover the window, and the highway. Then he would go to my brother's and sister's school, and when they were at recess, he would shoot them and their brains would repaint slides and the swing sets a brand new coat of red. Their blood would splatter onto the uniforms of their school mates. We would all be dead, and it would be my fault. Trevor was so good at painting a picture, a disturbing canvass of fear that escorted me to school each and every weekday morning.

Thank goodness I made it to Saturday. I looked forward to each and every Saturday morning. I would awake at 5 a.m. I would exercise and then eat my favorite breakfast: waffles with butter pecan ice cream and syrup-YUMMY! On Saturdays I could be a teenager. I could turn on my cartoons, and I could not wait for the clock to hit 7 a.m., so I could call Dade.

Dade was a local hockey jock. He was 16 years old but I swear he had the maturity of a 12-year-old, which constantly kept me entertained. I thought he was hilarious, and he seemed to appreciate his humor as well. I would call him on Saturday mornings and listen to him and his hockey buddies talk about the night on the ice and call each other superhero names. When I called he would say. "Hello. This is he-man here."

I played along and said this is "She-ra." I would listen to Dade and his buddies Erin and Sam put on their little comedy show. I looked forward to hearing their playfulness. I looked forward to my teenage Saturdays. I would laugh so hard at Dade that doll would flutter and kick to remind me that Erin, Dade and Sam were normal teenagers. They had fun. They played sports, and they thought they were talking to an innocent private school girl on the other line.

They were blind to the fact that I was a woman, a soon-to-be mother.

By 7:45 I was sure to hang up with Dade as I knew the beast would arise at 8 a.m., and if I did not call him at 8 a.m. he would begin his calling campaign. For some reason he could tell when he called me if I was on the other line, so thankfully I made sure I was off the phone with Dade in order to call Trevor on time. I never told Dade the real story. He was a happy teenage boy, and I was grateful that he gave me 45 minutes a week to be a teenage girl.

My 8 a.m. call to Mr. Broken followed the same pattern every time. He would answer on the first ring. On Saturdays he slept in because he had to get up early on the weekdays to stalk me. Ah, the life of a stalker, so hard so exhausting.

But this Saturday, I was a minute late. He answered the phone without saying hello and said, "See, bitch, you are late. I am going to kill your mother, your brother and your sister, and then finally your stupid pregnant ass."

Had he not gotten the memo that I was a genius? Before he could kill me, I would kill myself and come visit him in his dreams... well. I hoped his nightmares. I would brush him on the cheek and whisper in his ear "I won!" Ah, the victories we win in dreams of death that we just cannot manage to accomplish in life.

I said, "Well, good morning, Trevor. Don't you want to say hello before you go on your killing spree? I am sorry my mother was on the phone and I had to wait for her to get off. She was late going to her Saturday appointments. I am sorry Trevor."

The conversation turned normal and for a moment he sounded like a normal human being telling me how he was going to spend the day with Thomas, Keith and Juan. I did a victory dance in my room. Juan and the guys were the one thing that gave me a reprieve from Trevor's constant attention. Trevor asked me to hold on because there was a breaking news story on channel 12 (What the hell were they still doing in business?).

I turned my TV to Channel 12. Even though I was boycotting them, I had to see what had Trevor so intrigued and took his mind off of me. Maybe I could record it and he could watch that all of the time and forget about me. I was desperate. I would try anything.

"Last night there was a fatal bike accident on Lake Street. The young male on a motorcycle was travelling 100 miles per hour and hit a car head on. The male was ejected into the air and landed on his neck, which was instantly broken and the male was found by police dead on the scene. The young male is identified as Juan McEvers."

Trevor said, "Call Juan's house and find out if it is true. They have to have made a terrible mistake." I heard the desperation in his voice and conferenced in Juan's mother.

His mother's shaken voice said, "I am so sorry, sweetie. We lost Juan last night. He is dead." We both cried on the line, but for different reasons. She was crying because she lost her son, and I was crying because Trevor's main distraction from me was now gone. We both cried and we both apologized to each other. She did not know why she was apologizing to me but still she felt the need to apologize.

I released her from the line, and I heard Trevor sobbing on the other line. All I could think about was "Damn, he will not be hanging out with Juan today so we will have more time to bother me."

I was mad at Juan for dying now. Trevor would have more time to concentrate on me.

Trevor said he had to go.

I hung up and I said out loud "Juan, you selfish bastard. How dare you die and give him more time to get on my last nerve?"

Trevor called me back sobbing so hard on the other line saying "Juan! Why did you have to die?" I listened to him, cry and sob and scream, and say "Why Juan, why?"

I said under my breath "Yeah, why Juan, why?" I sat on the phone and listened to Trevor scream, and wail, as doll kicked me on the inside with her peaceful flutters of life, as Mr. Broken struggled with death's sudden hand on the other side.

Once again Trevor said he had to go.

HALLELUJAH!! Juan, your death might not be such a bad thing. I smiled, hung up the phone, and jumped for joy. *This maniac is so sad over the loss of his friend; he cannot be bothered with harassing me. Free at last.*

I called my friend Sarah and said "The beast has been tranquilized. Come pick me up in an hour."

I pulled the tags off of my new Levi jeans and slid on a pink backless halter top and sprayed on my mom's Burberry perfume. My stomach was no longer a 6 pack but a pouch which held my doll. I looked like I needed to do some sit ups, but the rest of my body was a masterpiece. I was beautiful, free, and flying.

Sarah pulled up with her curly blonde hair grazing the middle of her back. She said, "You look HOT, and it looks like you have actually gotten some sleep. I guess your jailer, Trevor, and your lover, calculus, have given you a break."

"Sarah my lover calculus is bringing me places that I have never seen before. There is more of him to go around Sarah. For some reason you just can't get over your lover, Mr. Algebra. I guess you are afraid of a challenge that a lover like calculus can bring to your life. Sarah, before I change my mind and curl up with my calculus book, get me out of here while I have some free time."

"Let's occupy your free time with Alex, I told him about you and he wants to meet you."

"Uh, Sarah, if you do not want to see Alex's cute face riddled with bullet holes courtesy of Trevor, you will keep him away from me. I am deadly to be around, like nuclear gas. "

"Will you ever just stand up for yourself? You cannot take this forever."

"Oh, Sarah, it feels like forever already. It is like God is punishing me for all the fire alarms that I pulled and all the tuna fish sandwiches I hid in my toy chest when I was elementary school. Maybe he is punishing me for the times I crushed up Smarties candies into a fine powder and snorted them up my nose through a straw like cocaine. Oh and not to mention what I did to those poor nuns in that Catholic school. I just know they were planning an exorcism event with my name on it. Sarah, I'm pregnant."

"Yikes. You cannot stay that way!"

"My grandmother calls it 'the family way'. Well, Sarah, this is not the way I dreamed my family would be. For some strange reason my dreams never included a psychopath."

"You do not even look pregnant. Well, your stomach is not the perfect six pack it usually is, so I am happy. I look more pregnant than you and I am not pregnant. You look great, so just have fun tonight. Alex is so hot and he is not worried about Trevor bullying him around. Trevor uses his strength and size against you, but Alex can step up to the challenge."

"Oh, Alex has the power to repel bullets? I must meet this superman. Why Sarah, I did not know I was meeting the man of steel. I must go re-powder my nose, I am meeting a superhero."

Sarah rolled her eyes and said, "Are you going to get in the car or are you going to sit here and dream up comic book fantasies?"

Alex was hotter than hot! He opened the door and said, "WOW, you are beautiful. Sarah said you were pretty, but I cannot believe someone as hot as you is at my door."

"Well Alex as hot as you think that I am, it is freezing outside." I smiled so hard I brought some sunshine to that dark night. I walked into his place. He rented the basement from his parents. He was seventeen. He had graduated early and was working as a manager at the upscale men's clothing store in the mall. Alex was beautiful. All I could do was smile, until my nose caught the scent of the pizza that he ordered. I was starving but how could I eat in front of Mr. Beauty pants?

Saturday night, my best friend and a hot guy-with pizza on top. This was the life! What would make it even better would be to finish my AP history paper before the weekend was over; I was so ready to tackle the events from the Boston Tea party to the American Revolution. For some reason I felt that I had THE paper, THE paper that would revolutionize AP history essays for centuries to come. I was ready to get home and write. I was excited I was free.

After a few hours of playing video games and eating pizza, Sarah brought me home. As Sarah pulled onto my street, I turned my head to look at the end of the cul-de-sac. I prayed I would not see his car waiting there. God heard my prayer before I even asked.

I headed down to my room and slid out my jeans into my favorite pink fleece pajamas. Those things were made to withstand the Arctic (When I bought them I was considering a move to the Arctic. I found out that Trevor hated the cold, I decided a residence there would not be too bad.) Once I had donned on fleece, I made hot chocolate and sat down to type. Right in the middle of my historical masterpiece the phone rang. I answer on the first ring.

"He is a fucking maniac!"

"Sarah?"

"How did you find this lunatic?"

"Sarah, I never had lunatics on my list of finders' keepers. Calm down and stop screaming. I can't understand you."

"After I dropped you off, I stopped at the red light; Trevor zoomed in front me and cut me off so I could not pass him. He jumped out the car and started banging on my window. I thought if I opened the door hard enough, I could knock him over. When I opened the door he pulled me by my hair and held my hand behind my back. He said he would break my arm if I did not tell him who you were with this evening. I told him he already knew who you were with me. He said, 'Stop being the dumb bitch for once in your life and tell me what guy you were with.'

I said, 'Well, you should know. You were following us the whole night. How do you have time? Shouldn't you be helping your best friend's mom plan his funeral?"

I lost my breath. "What? He followed us? I did not see him following us at all."

"You were not looking for him. You were so excited to be out and away from him, you did not once turn your head to see if he was following us. I was going to show the dumb jerk that we were going to have fun tonight, so if wanted to waste his gas driving around following us, then so be it."

"Sarah, Sarah! You could have told me you saw him. Trevor is crazy and he could have killed everyone there."

"He has knocked your brains out! He only wants to fight girls. He is too weak to stand up to someone who can fight back and win. You fight back but you can't win."

"Sarah call the police. Maybe if they hear it from you they will believe you."

"I am not calling the police; I am not calling the police. I told my parents and they said they don't want any trouble, and YOU are trouble and a bad influence. They want me to stay away from you. I am sorry. I will see you in school.

She hung up. She was gone, and I was trouble.

The phone rang. I answered. "Bitch," Trevor said. The phone rang. I answered. "Bitch." The phone rang. I answered. "Bitch, I'm going to kill you."

At least he'd said more than "bitch" that time.

50 times the phone rang. 47 times I heard, "Bitch I am going to kill you." Every time the phone rang I knew what words would greet me on the other line, I knew the words were meant for me, I was getting the custom message for trouble makers, courtesy of Trevor. "Bitch, I am going to kill you."

I felt numb. I felt crazy. Life was moving fast, it was unforgiving.

***

That Monday I left school early and began walking down Lake Street.

Every couple of feet there were crosses and roses and bears, memorials to Juan. I guessed the memorial was every couple of feet, as parts of Juan's body had been distributed throughout the street upon impact. It ripped his body to shreds. I was so angry with his demise. It was his fault. He kept Trevor distracted from me until he went and got himself killed. Maybe he wanted to kill himself so that he, too, could escape Trevor. Maybe Trevor beat his friends, too, and maybe Juan would rather be splattered across Lake Street than have to be around Trevor ever again. I was so mad at Juan for whatever reason he left life, whether it was his decision or God's. At every memorial I said "F**k you, Juan"

One of the girls from Juan's high school heard me and said, "YOU ARE CRAZY. Who looks at someone's memorial and curses them? Are you a lunatic? You are so cruel to do this! You are a miserable person! I hope YOU die!!"

I said, "You are completely right, and I hope so too!" I heard the girl's screams and curses at me as I walked away. Yes, I was officially crazy.

It was our anniversary. "Let's go to get you your favorite food!" Trevor was overjoyed. "You are pregnant. You need to eat, plus it's our anniversary!"

I rolled my eyes. (What guy actually remembers an anniversary?).

"It has been a year since I made you mine." I rolled my eyes, then smiled "Yes, 'made' is correct. Let's have a toast to my yearlong misery." I rose up an imaginary glass and said "CHEERS!!" I saw his heart break in that moment. It seemed to look like little red pellets on the floor until I looked down and saw those blood pellets flowing from my lips onto the ground. I cursed my mistaken mind to think that I broke the monster's heart, those pellets that I thought were from his broken heart were actually my blood from his fist. My face had become so numb from being hit so many times. I did not even know the difference.

Then I heard the footsteps of Trevor's Aunt Maya and Uncle Todd creak up the stairs. Oh, joy they came to join in the anniversary fun!

"Trevor, PLEASE keep your hands off of that girl!"

I thought to myself in that moment *That girl?* I might be a punching bag, but I was more than *That girl*. Then I thought maybe I was one of many that Trevor brought home to torture and I was just a number. I cannot believe that at the time I was that upset by her not realizing my relevance. I guessed being beaten up makes who you are, your soul, your being, no longer relevant.

And as if I needed further confirmation that Trevor was an unstoppable psychopath he said "Shut up, Maya, and mind your F** business Todd, you need to handle your wife, because she is taking this bitch's side"

Wow, I went from *that girl* to *bitch* and Uncle Todd and Aunt Maya lost the respect of being called Aunt and Uncle. This was some hella'versary.

### Unforgiven

I got my report card. All A's. There was a note from the Spanish teacher that said, "Due to Zara's effort and hard work her lowest quiz grade was replaced by her grade for written essay about author Gabriel Garcia Marquez." My math teacher wrote "Zara was able to earn 50 extra calculus points through her participation in the math-a-thon."

Oh, yes, the math-a-thon. As soon as I walked out of the math-a-thon, Trevor's car was front and center outside of the building. I walked to his car and I said "Hey I will give you an math problem and if you get it wrong you have to never contact me again. If you get it right then I will keep being your girlfriend and I will even act happy about it." I got in the car and I created the longest most complex math problem I could. He smiled and said he would try it when we got to his house.

When we got to his house, we sat right at the table and he began to try and break down the problem. He had a scientific calculator and everything. I thought to myself, *Why does he have one of these? Only students have scientific calculators and he dropped out of school. What does he want to do, look like a student?* He also carried a backpack, so I guess he liked the accessories; he just did not want to attend school.

I watched him struggle through the problem that I set him up for him to fail. I took such joy in his struggle. I loved that he would fail and I would be free. I would earn my freedom with what I knew best - MATH. I loved that I was smarter than he. Even if he killed me he could not kill the knowledge inside of me. I watched him struggle and sweat and try really hard. I began to daydream about my days without him. One minute he was working rigorously with the calculator. The next minute he was scribbling on the paper, he was really trying and he finally asked, "What is the answer?"

I looked at him confused. "If you cannot do math, you should go to school. I win! We agreed that if you could not solve the problem we could break up, so I am sorry I cannot give you the answer." And then for some reason I smiled.

It was as if the smile somehow ignited a cannon of calculators, pencils, papers, glasses, chairs and shoes to be targeted at my head. I fell the floor to cover my head and to ball myself up to protect doll.

Trevor stopped throwing things and began kicking me. As he focused on kicking me in my stomach I focused on protecting my doll. He shouted, "Whose baby is this? Ryan's? Alex's?"

Somehow, I found a way to catch my breath; I screamed back, "This baby is MINE!!MINE!"

Then he pulled me up and dropped to his knees and put his arms around my waist and began this heaving cry. "Please. Help me. PLEEEEEESE HELP ME." He cried so hard and held me tight. I rubbed his arm, and he sobbed some more. He cried again "Please. Help me, but no police." His cries made his body tremble as he held me by my waist.

I was tired. I was sore, and as he cried I felt the tickle of doll's feet in my stomach and I joined Trevor in his trembling cry for help. That moment we cried in unsaid agreement that we were both caged and that our pleas for help were to be set free from the prison called "Trevor."

I cried myself to sleep, and I felt Trevor lift me up onto the bed. After a deep warm sleep I woke up to find myself lying on the bed with my arms folded across my chest with Trevor staring and smiling at me. He said softly, "You make a beautiful dead person."

My God! Trevor had staged me to see how I would look in a coffin.

## Cry Baby

The next day I went to school with bloodshot eyes and a busted vessel in my eye. I remembered this was the day I was campaigning for class president. I wrote my speech in ten minutes. Since I had an overwhelmingly bubbly personality my victory was pretty much a given. Maria, Sarah, Tina, and Aya were my best friends. We made sure that we hung out at lunch everyday. That day Maria asked that we skip lunch and just talk in the school auditorium. She was so beautiful. She was my soft spoken friend whose beauty spoke loud and clear.

The tears flowed from her big brown eyes. I looked at her and tried to hug her. I was worried about her. I asked her "Has someone hurt you?"

She shook her head and looked at me and said, "No, someone is hurting you."

My blood boiled. I was so angry at her. I wanted to slap her for crying. How dare she cry? How did this all work? Trevor used me as a punching bag, and he got to cry, Maria gave me a tearful stare for 20 minutes and she got to cry, yet no one laid a finger on her beautiful face. And she is crying? How is it that the one who was getting beaten was not crying? "Look at your eyes; look at your face. You need to leave Trevor alone. I know he is beating you like he beat his last girlfriend."

Maria, do you think I want to be with Trevor. I have no choice. It is either be with him or die, and have my family killed too. You have offered me no help, no way out, nothing but your useless tears."

She screamed "I care, and I don't want you hurt anymore."

"Well, Maria it is not my choice to be hurt, but this is my life. It honestly does not hurt anymore. What hurts is my so called friends making this about them." I walked away from her.

Trevor had to take his uncle on errands, which bought me a free pass for the day. I got home and the phone rang. I answered and it was a shaky female voice. "Hi, Zara, this is Tania, Trevor's ex-girlfriend."

"Oh the girl from the bag! How can I help you?"

"I wanted to warn you about Trevor."

At that moment I broke out into the most thunderous laugh ever. "Warn me? Warn me? Your warning is way too late. I do not even want to hear your too late warning. What I do need is your help. I need you to go to the police with me and tell them what happened."

"The police? No way, Trevor is crazy and he is finally leaving me alone because he is occupied with you. I am not getting involved."

I had just finished reading my history of feminism book and was all pumped about how women unite to fight against the odds, yet I saw no one wanted to unite to help me escape Trevor. After I hung up on Tania, the phone rang. It was Trevor. "WHO ARE YOU ON THE PHONE WITH?!"

"Trevor I was not on the phone."

"I just saw Ryan getting off of the bus that comes from your area."

I laughed "You did? Did you tell him I said hello?"

"You are such a smart ass Bitch! I swear I know for a fact that is Ryan's baby and I am going to kill you and his baby!" Then he hung up on me.

I sat on my bed and I tried to muster up some tears. I wanted to feel bad for me. I wanted to cry. I couldn't. All I could do was plan. Plan to win. Trevor wanted to hurt doll even more than he wanted to hurt me. I had done so well protecting her, but when she was no longer in my belly he would be able to get to her. That day I chose between taking a chance of never being forgiven by God or seeing my baby killed at the hands of a psychopath. Which one was more unforgivable? Knowing when this baby came it would suffer at the hands of Trevor, or making sure my doll did not suffer at all. Then the tears came. I felt everyone just failed me - my mom, my friends, my dad and my God and most of all I had failed me, but I would not fail doll.

I walked into the women's center to do the only thing I knew would protect her from Trevor. They said that I was too far along and that I would need a judge's permission for a late termination. Due the fact that I was a minor I would need to get special permission. They said they would have to put off giving me a full examination and time was of the essence.

I said, "I may be a minor but I am dealing with a major maniac."

The woman held my hand in hers and she said you will also need a money order for $1000.00.

Sure Ma'am, I will draw that right from my Swiss bank account.

She informed me about a fund that "helps women in danger and in turmoil." And then I went to went to the courthouse and obtained permission to rip out my soul. The answer was yes, the fund would help me pay to do what in my mind was unforgivable. I went to the FUND. I asked myself who funds this fund? Women who have dated men like Trevor?

I still needed 300 dollars. I looked at my wrist and my ring. Staring at the bracelet and the ring somehow zapped me into the pawn shop. I handed them my ring, bracelet and necklace. They handed me 500.00 dollars. They next day I was approved for independent study. I went to the clinic for my checkup. I walked in and I asked the lady who told me about the Fund, about Adoption. I told her I needed to find a way to keep doll from Trevor. She said that first I would need a full examination and then we could go back and discuss all options.

As I lay on the crinkly white paper in the office, the doctor put cold jelly on my stomach and then rolled what seemed like a computer mouse over my stomach. "Have you felt any fetal movement?"

"Fetal movement?" I said, "What is that?"

"When is the last time you felt the baby move?"

I could not remember the last time I felt the baby move. I was tired and hungry because I had only eaten a Greek yogurt in two days. I did not remember that last time that I felt doll.

"I see a fetus, but there is no heartbeat and no fetal movement."

I said to the doctor, "That's okay, isn't it? My heart is beating. If the baby eats what I eat, doesn't my heart beat for her?" I tried to think really hard about what biology said about reproduction. My brain was frozen, and again the "genius" did not have any answer.

The doctor then said, "The fetus is not viable and we need to induce labor."

I did not understand what the doctor was saying. All I could think about was how I'd failed Doll. I'd failed to protect her. I'd failed to keep her heart beating.

The next day I pulled the classic get out of school free card. "Mommy, I have a sore throat." She left and took my brother and sister to the sitter, and of course Trevor was outside waiting. When my mother drove off, I walked to the car and told him that something was wrong and my doctor told me to report to the hospital. When I got to the hospital I was examined again by the doctor. He confirmed "No fetal heartbeat, no fetal movement."

They immediately tried to stick a needle in my veins but had trouble because I was so dehydrated. They induced labor and I delivered my Doll. They wrapped up my Doll in a white blanket and carried her away. She was still not moving just like the baby dolls I used to play with, and along with my stuffed animals, still adorned my bed. They wrapped her up and carried her away.

As they took my doll away I turned to Trevor and looked at his teary eyes. Again I wondered to myself how the hell he got to cry!

He looked at the ground and said: "I will never hit you again. I am sorry. I need help. I pressed the button so the nurse attendant could hear the *I'm sorry*, so someone official would know, I would have a witness. But of course my brilliant plan was ruined when she shouted "How may I help you?" Trevor stopped his apologetic confession and became tight lipped.

I felt so empty. I felt so wrong. I needed my rosary. I needed to say my penance, all my Hail Marys. How dare I pray to Mary, the purest woman of all women? I was undeserving. She was full of God's grace and I was full of unworthiness, unworthy of God's forgiveness. My heart was black and I was numb. I'd earned my commandment-breaking stripes. The doctor came in and said that I would need to rest for a few hours. I lay down and felt heavy with emptiness. I felt like a monster, just like Trevor. I looked at him and smiled. He was crying, tired, scared and broken. I reached for his hand and he placed his in mine. Through my wide smile I whispered "I forgive you. I am you."

## My Escape

The next day, Trevor did not call me. I had no doll, I had no friends, no Ryan; just me. I decided I would spend the day with me. After days of not feeling the desire to eat at all I felt like some tacos and ice cream from the mall would make me feel better. I also wanted to visit the new book store and get a book of James Joyce poems and another copy of "Things Fall Apart." My mother dropped me off at the mall. As I ate my tacos, my shirt suddenly became wet. It was soaked. I went in the bathroom and changed into the new tank tops I'd bought. As I stood in line for my ice cream, my shirt was wet again and dripping down my arm was a watery cloudy sticky liquid. A woman standing next to me in line said, "Oh did you just have a baby? You are leaking! Where is your baby? Your body is telling you it's time to feed the baby." There was no baby to feed yet my body wanted to actually do something good for Doll. It was too late. And there it began the stream of tears and the stream of milk from my breast.

When I got home I threw all of my stuffed animals and dolls in a bag and set them in the trash in the garage. And then the phone rang, I answered on the first ring "Bitch why haven't you called me all day?"

I hung up the phone and turned all the ringers on silent. He could have called all night and I would not have known and I did not care.

On my third sick day from school, my mom, brother, and sister had been gone for hours. There was a ring at the doorbell. I looked outside the door and there was a box. I guess Fed Ex just dropped off the box. I opened the door and grabbed the box. I felt a hand grab my neck and I was thrown into the doorway onto the floor. With no words Trevor slammed me into the wall and then dragged me up the stairs to the kitchen. He threw me on the ground and began kicking me. I felt myself screaming. He pulled me up by my hair and I felt some of my hair come out. I grabbed Trevor's arm and he bit me. As I ripped my arm from his mouth I felt as though I was in a fight with a rabid dog.

He slammed me against the counter, and my body knocked over my mom's new set of glasses. I fell to the floor screaming. Without a word Trevor walked out the door. I looked at the time. It was 2:00 p.m. I said to myself, "I need to clean up before my mother gets home"

I took a shower and brushed my hair back to cover up my new bald spot. Another blood vessel had burst in my eye and I had bite marks and bruises on my arm. I looked like a horror movie.

I sat down to write my speech for the student council presidency. I could not think of any words. I did not deserve to win anything. I felt the only thing that I deserved was the long death sentence that I'd lived through for two years. I stood looking at the blank sheet of paper. I heard the words of a song, "You can win as long as you keep your head to the sky--be optimistic."

And there was my speech that would take someone in a horror movie and make her into student council president the very next day.

That same day I decided that I had won--something.   And if it was time to die it was okay.  But no matter how many times Trevor called the school dance room phone; I would keep dancing and ignore him.  I practiced my routine in the large dance mirror, with my bruises, bite marks and busted blood vessels in my eyes.  I looked at myself and I continued to dance and if it was time for me to die, I was ready.  As long as I did not have to deal with Trevor I would accept death.

As I danced, the door opened, and there stood Trevor.  Even though my mind said I was ready to die my heart still feared death.  I ran through the set design room and up through the back entrance to the stage.  The set design room was a maze, and Trevor would take a while to figure out where he was.

I ran into the Dean's Office and I screamed, "HE IS GOING TO KILL ME!!"  She ran in two different directions like a squirrel, and she said, "Who is trying to kill you?" as she called the police.  Of course when Woodbridge School calls the police they manage to be there in seconds.  It seemed like it took only a few like minutes until they walked up the stairs with Trevor.  He saw me and started pleading, "Please don't do this. I just wanted to talk!"

### The Prom

Thank God for springtime!  A summer without Trevor in it is a good summer indeed.  I was looking forward to it.  Trevor's mom was told by Woodbridge that if Trevor ever contacted me, or was located within 100 feet of me or Woodbridge she would be fired.  Sarah and Maria now spent their days trying to keep my mind off of the past and told me not to be upset with them; they had just wanted me to be okay.

As soon as I had that thought the phone rang. My heart sank right into my stomach. As it rang, I imagined Trevor deciding he was just going to go flat out radical and berserk and ignore the restraining order.  I still do not understand how a piece of paper is supposed to "restrain" someone.  I had slyly suggested to the judge "I think handcuffs or a straightjacket would be much more efficient."  At that point the judge suggested I get some counseling.  I thought to myself *I may need counseling but he may need a few more years of schooling to think that a piece of paper can restrain a monster.*

The ringing stopped and my heart seemed to float back up to my chest.  As soon as it got snuggled back in its chamber the phone rang again and there my heart went, plummeting to its new stomach home. I snatched up the receiver and the shaky teenager boy's chipper voice cleared and said, "Can I speak to Zara?"

I said, "This is she."

"This is Clarence."

"Hey what's up?"  Clarence was the guy I went to the semi-formal with.  My family adored him.  He was the community good boy, the boy that girl's mothers would love them to date and to marry.  If my mother knew he was calling me she would be hearing wedding bells instead of the phone ring. I could never understand why Clarence would not face the fact that he could not dance. He jerked around like he had a lizard in his pants instead of sliding into the "Keep my cool two-step, or the head banger head nod." But nooo he had to be an overachiever. He was as close to Jesus as you can get so no need for him to keep failing at dancing. Before I burst into laughing from my vision of him dancing, I was awakened by his asking me if I would like to go to his senior prom. HALLELUJAH, I was NORMAL. I was going to the prom!

"YES, I will go."

"Hey, by the way, will you be my girlfriend?" My heart started to beat so fast. I was going to be normal, an all A student, an athlete, and dating the star baseball player at the best high school in the area. He had a car and Mommy would let me go anywhere he wanted to go because he was such a good boy. YES! She had kept me under lock and key just in case Trevor the monster became unrestrained. Through all that hell she seemed to trust me more. "Okay, I will be your girlfriend."

"Hey I have one question. You still don't talk to the guy who used to beat you, do you?"

"Oh, yes, I love to talk to him. He is my best friend. I tell him I just can't wait till the next beating. Idiot! I changed my mind I do not want to be your girlfriend."

"I am so sorry. I did not mean to offend. I just wanted to make sure you were safe."

"When is this prom so I can ask my mother?"

"May 21st."

"That is two weeks from now. By then I will decide if I will be your girlfriend."

My mother was thrilled. She jumped up and down laughing and smiling.

"Umm, would you like to go in my place?'

"Don't be a wise ass, but then again that would be like asking you to not breathe. I am just happy for you I want the best for you, and he is the best, so show me some respect."

We went to the mall and instantly found a white strapless A-line dress. We also purchased a tight swimsuit-looking bodysuit to go under the dress so it would have a smooth fit.

The next thing I knew I woke up it was prom day.

**8 a.m.**, hair salon.

**12 p.m.**, nail salon.

**2 p.m.**, makeup artist.

**4 p.m.**, back to nail salon, as I had managed to break off all of the fake nails.

**6 p.m.**, get stuffed into dress.

**6:15 p.m.**, Doorbell rings for me to step into normal and be escorted to the prom in a stretch white limo. All that was missing was the carriage and the white horses.

My whole family came. They were so happy. All the neighbors came too. They all snapped pictures of me pinning a flower in his tuxedo jacket and me holding the beautiful red roses he'd brought me.

I could not breathe. The dress was too tight. I did not like him, and the damn thorns form the roses were pricking my arms.

He opened the door to the limo and I fell back into the seat because I could not bend my body so I just fell into the seat. He talked about baseball and bases and college scholarships and where he would be attending in the fall. I thought to myself, there will be no third base here, buddy. I learned his whole life story in a 30 minute ride.

The prom dining and dancing room was beautiful. There were white chandeliers that seemed to shine right on me. I fell into my seat and I listened to all the girls talk about how long the hair took and where they got their dresses from and how they had to get a smaller size and not eat for a week before the prom.

Hmm maybe that was why I could not breathe. I had pizza, oodles of noodles and yogurt. I was pretty curvy, yet the dress refused to let my curves breathe.

The conversation was about going to the mall, and the movies and all the fun days of high school. I did not know those days. At my plays I performed in I was stalked, at my school dance recitals I was stalked, at my field hockey games he stood there holding his arm in his jacket letting me know he had a gun.

They talked about their rides on the school bus and how fun they were and how they finally had cars. I thought of my mentally treacherous rides to school being followed. They talked about their high school loves and how they would call them and whisper sweet nothings. I thought about the phone calls, being yelled at, hung up on, called back, yelled at, hung up on, called back, yelled at, hung up on.... I could not breathe. This prom is not me. I could not breathe. This was not my life. This was not my reality. I did not belong there.

Then the conversation turned to me. "So, hey, your dress is really cute. So you look okay now," one of the girls said to me. She had long red hair and beautiful bright blue eyes. Her name was Tara.

"What do you mean by I look okay now. Did I have the flu, the chicken Pox?"

"I mean you look okay, no scars no bruises"

"Bruises? I mean I think this dress is a little tight but uh, bruises?"

Jenna butted in. "Is Tara mistaken? Aren't you that girl whose boyfriend used to beat her?"

I looked at Clarence. He just stood there. I looked to him to say something, anything, maybe change the subject to baseball, his scholarships, awaken the lizard and start dancing, something. He said nothing.

I could not breathe. I was being squeezed by the embarrassment of being the girl who was beaten. I did not belong here at the prom for the normal kids. I was defeated. No wonder this dress didn't fit. It was NOT customized for me. The designer forgot to embroider the scarlet letter B-for beaten girl.

"This fucking dress is choking me" I screamed

I ripped off the dress, down to the body suit that was supposed to give the dress a smooth fit. Yet when I ripped the dress off, I could finally breathe. I looked down at myself. I looked at the swimsuit garment and then I looked at my heels.

I ran out in my heels and my swimsuit to the stretch white limo. I hoped I was in the right limo. I would be even more embarrassed that I ripped off my dress down to the undergarment and then jumped in the wrong limo.

I knew I was in the right limo when Clarence jumped in the limo and began to scream at me." You ruined my prom! You embarrassed me!"

When I arrived at home there was a message from Dade.

"Hey, I was thinking that we should hang out this summer before I leave for school. Freshman orientation is this weekend and when I return, let's have dinner."

I deleted the message. I did not want to embarrass Dade. I wanted to save him from the antics of the "beaten girl." I slammed the phone against the wall. "Bright idea Dade, decide to date me when you are leaving for college!" Who was I screaming at? I was alone, and that is how I wanted to stay. I never wanted to date anyone again. I wanted to be free. I wanted to only be responsible for loving me and only me.

The realization came upon me. I made myself believe that it was my fault that I was known as the beaten girl. It was my fault. I hated me. I should have listened to my mother. Trying to control my life and create what I thought was normal threw me into a tailspin of misery. The people in the town said that I was bad, that I was a "fast and loose girl" and I believed them. At every turn I tried to create the life I wanted by manipulating things into what I wanted them to be. Thank God every step of the way God was pulling me closer to him.

***

The phone rang and woke me out of the daze of loss. I let it go to voicemail. When I listened, it was Aunt Sandy. Her voice always sounds like she is smiling. Every time one of my aunts would call me, I instantly went from feeling like a loser to feeling like a princess. When they called their voice always sounded like they were happy that they were responsible for making me smile. I have a lot of aunts and a lot of smiles. "Hi honey this is your auntie just remember that you are a genius and I just wanted you to know you are such a gift to this family."

### Tight, Tough, Tender and Tense

As I continued on my journey I realized that God will place people in my path to encourage me on the way. On a fall evening, I looked across the street and I saw the one who inspired me to put my pain on paper. There she was, the one that inspired me to share with the world that me and my story exist; and the world deserves to know my story no matter how horrible and unforgivable it is.

I walked up to her and I screamed: MAYA ANGELOU! I could barely catch my breath between words. She had just completed a performance in the city and God saw it fit for me to see her entering her hotel. I told her that she inspired me and I wanted to be just like her. I wanted to inspire, I wanted to give others peace through my work. I wanted to be important. She put my face in her hands and spoke to me through a crooked, beautiful smile in a deep voice.

"My dear always remember to be TIGHT, TOUGH, TENDER AND TENSE"

In that moment I remembered what my grandmother told me. She said I was beautifully and wonderfully made in God's image. That no one had the right to hurt me, no matter what mistakes I have made; I was a child of God. I had relied on my earthly father to protect me, to prioritize me and when he died I felt helpless. It was true, I needed help. I spun out of control because of loss, the need for acceptance and the inability to let go. My fear of Trevor captured me and made me blame myself for all the times he beat me. He was broken and he successfully broke me down to believing that the paths I chose made me deserve to be abused. That could not be further from the truth. I realized that I am a woman. God said that I am more precious than rubies. Once I accepted that, I felt the world at my feet. God was elevating me, I closed my eyes, released control and let him lead.

"On the warm day in September
God gave me a reason to remember
I am beautifully and wonderfully made
For my sins he has already paid
I am made in his image
and as I hold my baby girl
I realize…
I AM FORGIVEN"-Wendashia Ray

# Victory
## Imagined Possibilities by Tamara E. Stallings

"I'm a promise, I'm a possibility, I'm a promise with a Capital P, I'm a promise to be anything God wants me to be." Singing this song in Ms. Herron's class during the second grade meant very little to me at the time. It wouldn't have much significance in my life until years later. Today, as a matter of fact. *Can I really do this?* I ask myself again; Then again. Out loud this time, only slower, *CAN I REAL-LY DO THIS?* I mean, I'm just a girl from south central Los Angeles. Staring at myself intently in the mirror. Watts to be exact. I'm not light skinned, nor do I have long, straight hair down to my ass. Well, I do, but, I didn't grow it from my own head. Oh, snap, do I have dead lady hair? Aw hell, naw, I got dead lady hair. Shit, I let these white people talk me into...

"Peyton, are you in here?" She whispers... loudly. "Peyton".

This time, I sigh. "Yes, I am. I'm almost done." I just have to wash my hands. Shit, I hope she didn't hear me. My mother-in-law, Janice. So sweet and a great supporter on my journey. More than I can say for my own family.

"Girl, are you crying?"

"No," I say, "just going over my talking points."

"Here, let me help you," she says. "I am so proud of you, sweetie. If your mother was here," she continues, "Well, hmph, she'd be so proud of you."

I say nothing as she holds my chin and looks me in the eye. "There, all done. Turn around; let me see you."

I do as she says.

"You look amazing. Just amazing, Miss Global Senior Vice President.

One last look in the mirror. I hear the MC introducing me...introducing the new Senior Global Vice President of Yerian, Inc, Mrs. **Peyton Michele Allensworth**. As I step into the ballroom onto the stage, I see my village beaming with pride. My husband, father-in-law, sorority sisters, cousins, they're all here, cheering, nodding their heads with approval, as I approach the podium. This little chocolate girl with the sassy mouth, the C student, the big dreamer has finally made it.

I was born to be great. I've always known that. At pinnacle times in my life, what I have always felt and instinctively knew was confirmed in some way, form or fashion. Like the time I completed the forms to attend a gifted school that was two hours away from my house. By the time I got the acceptance letter, my mother couldn't argue with the decision for me to go. Yes, I forged her signature but that's beside the point. We both wanted me out of the local junior high school in our community. I wanted out way more than she did. By the time the letter came, all she could say was "Pey, are you sure?" Yes, momma, I'm sure. You already signed the papers, anyway". Just relax. I will be okay.

"What's wrong with the local junior high school? You think you too good to go to the school down the street?" My brother always had something to say. I chose to ignore him because my mother already said that I could go. Even if she had said no, I was still going. I made sure of that because I had called the school to request that my records be transferred two weeks before. Going to that gifted school was one of the best things that ever happened to me. Kids at the gifted school weren't fighting and getting shot at every day. The teachers could actually teach without Michael little-bad-ass disrupting the class damn near daily. No more war zone for me. Most days, I only had to decide if I wanted pizza or chicken nuggets for lunch....most days. Every now and then I had to check a little white girl for a variety of things, but mostly, because of my own insecurities which loudly told me that I did not belong. When I felt like I was starting to belong, my insecurities changed. I belong but "they don't like me." A black girl from the hood had it hard in and out of the hood. The people in the hood...those close to you, don't understand why you're trying to get out, and those out of hood...those who are in the position that you're moving toward don't want you in. So I struggled on the outside of two worlds.

In spite of my struggles to fit in, I knew being at that school was God orchestrated. I knew, but I didn't know. It was a gut feeling that I had with visual reminders of the consequences of my future actions every day, like the neighborhood drunks on the corner waiting for the liquor store to open when I walked to school each morning, the stray dogs running through the neighborhood, limping on one leg with no place to go, just trying to survive, and the look of gloom in the community. Graffiti on the walls, trash in the street. The visual reminders were glaring. I was young but extremely intuitive. I knew my fate if I didn't aim higher.

I was often reminded of the greatness that was inside of me at different times in my life. I got just enough reminders from God to give me hope. A little bit more each time. Especially during those times when life was kicking my ass. Those times when I wanted to give up and when the tears were streaming sown my eyes, I would get a reminder snippet or a still small voice that said "keep going" The agony of not just arriving at my greatness felt like a sick joke was being played on me over and over again. I could see it, touch it, but I couldn't have or be it.

Greatness Reminder: "Sit down and don't touch nothing. I don't have no money to pay for anything that you break."

"Okay, Momma, I'm not going to touch anything," I say to her as I look around the massive museum. I don't know why Momma is here to clean this place. It already looks pretty clean to me. I dare not ask her that stupid question. She's still mad at me for being kicked off the school bus, which caused me to have to come to work with her today. Yes, I did tell the bus driver to shut up and drive, but isn't that what she's supposed to do? I mean, how can you bark at me for getting out of my seat to get candy from Christina AND pay attention to the road? That's how accidents happen. I thought I was helping her focus, but apparently, I was being insubordinate to the bus driver.

I sit in silence for a long time, staring at the grand piano, the beautiful paintings, the shiny black iron gate that separated the living room from the dining hall and the beautiful stained glass windows. I start day dreaming about owning a beautiful house just like this museum. I have a husband, two children, a nice car and a lot of money. In fact, we have three cars, and a pool in the backyard. We have a maid too. A wide smile comes across my face. My heart is racing as I think about being able to go to the finest restaurants every day - not the occasional Kentucky Fried Chicken meal that we got when Momma got a little extra money.

"Didn't I tell you not to touch anything?"

"I…I…uh, I was just seeing how it sounded."

"Don't TOUCH THE PIANO!"

I slowly move away from the piano in the opposite direction of where she stands. I'm not trying to get slapped today.

"Are you hungry, Pey?"

"Yes!" I say excitedly and thankfully to move on to my favorite topic. "Well, come on then." We head to the kitchen. "I wish we had a kitchen this size, Momma."

She ignores me. "Do you want turkey or ham on your sandwich?"

"Ham!" I say loudly, "With cheese!"

Momma spins around, looks me sternly in the eye. "Listen, I'm going to make this sandwich for you. Then you come upstairs with me so that I can finish cleaning this house and we can leave."

"This is a house, Momma? People live here? This is a big house. Why can't we live here?"

"Peetie, stop asking questions. Eat that sandwich so that I can finish my work."

I eat quietly; she sits and watches me until I finish the last bite. "Let's go!"

Upstairs, the rooms are more massive than downstairs. Each room noticeably kissed by the sun. The massive windows take my breath away. I'm in awe. I walk towards the window. I can see the Hollywood sign, I say. It's so close. If I just stretch myself a little, I can touch it, I tell myself.

"Take this and start vacuuming in that room over there."

I do as I'm told, all the while daydreaming that we were in MY house, in MY bedroom, vacuuming MY carpet. I open the closet door. *Look at all these clothes!* I've died and gone to heaven. My heart won't stop beating fast. And the shoes; How many pairs of shoes can a person own? I'm overwhelmed, dreaming out loud, in Technicolor of this worry-free, rich life. I can taste better with every deep inhale, from every corner of the room, from the high vaulted ceilings to the rich crown molding. Apparently I'm still daydreaming when…

"Here comes the bus!" I stand up quickly almost falling.

"Girl, you are so clumsy. What are you so deep in thought about?"

"Nothing," I say as I board the 92 bus and pay my $.90 cents fare that my momma gave to me, heading back to my reality.

***

I made it through high school. I'm not sure how, because I thought that I was a credit or two or twelve short but, thank you Jesus. I was graduating AND getting the fuck outta there. I needed and wanted to leave LA. I wish I was going off to college but college was not talked about much in my house. Even though I was in a "gifted" program, not much was said about college to me at school either. What else was I going to do? Get a job? Stay in the community? Most of the people on my block were in the neighborhood gang, had babies, and were on welfare, dead or close to dying. I didn't plan on fitting into any of those categories, so I made plans to go to the military in ninth grade. I wasn't smart enough to think that I could excel at college yet. Truth be told, I wasn't even sure what college was all about, seeing as nobody in my neighborhood went, except for one person. Michelle was three years older, one of twelve children, and my only real life example of tangible success. Our families were friends. We attended the same corner church. She started off at the local community college, then a four year college - Cal State Dominquez Hills. I could see a change in her too, almost immediately. She talked differently, walked differently. I was intrigued by her success. I often wondered what she was learning at that college when I'd see her get off the bus heading towards home. She looked like she was going places. She graduated from ghetto before my very eyes. She was a human confirmation that I wanted to join the class of people who graduated from urban living.

I had lots of friends from my white school who were going off to college; yet, I didn't know enough, so I used the military as my excuse. "I want to serve my country," was the lie I told myself and others. "I need discipline." Straight bullshit. I needed to get the fuck out of this town, pronto. There had to be MORE than this, more than waiting on a government check on the first and the 15th, more than borrowing sugar from the neighbor until the next check came, more than the lack ambition, the poor health and the…waiting to die. I refused to be a statistic and so, one August 24th at 6 p.m., I boarded the plane to my future, to work for my new employer. The U.S. Navy. The employer that I vowed I would never work for. Yeah, sure I was in ROTC in junior high and high school but this is real now. Not just a class. THIS WAS REAL. In my community, you did not go to the military. The military was not always good to black people. My stepfather was proof of that. He spent fifteen years in the military. Two wars later, all that he had to show for being in the military were endless trips to the VA Hospital, a thirty percent disability check and two amputated toes. But yet, here I am, going to work for….lay my life on the line for… ironic.

"Attention on Deck!" What The fuck?! It's August 20th, and I turn eighteen tomorrow. I was super excited, two days ago but now a loud Brutus looking motherfucka from Popeye's cartoon is banging on a trash can with the bright ass lights on. "Attention on deck!"

I'm scared to death and thinking *what the hell does "Attention on Deck" mean*, and actually don't tell me until after my birthday, because I don't really give a fuck.

"Get on the line!" I snap to, trying to figure out where this gawdt damn line is so that I can punch it in the eye, Watts, LA style. Does this fool know that it's 3a.m. and that it's my fucking birthday?

This is not how I planned to turn eighteen. Boot camp! I thought this was going to be a fun, life-changing decision. Joining the military that is. It's been less than twenty-four hours and I'm ready to go already. More yelling, more screaming from this crazy man…As the tears begin to fall down my face into my hands, temporarily staining the new shirt that I bought to celebrate my new journey, I now know fun is not what this will be.

"Get your ass up and drink this water until your bladder blows up and piss in this cup, numb nuts!" Life changing, yes. Fun? Not. It is strange that I've always been an extremely intuitive person. I silently vowed right then and there, not to stay in this shit.

*Count to ten, Peyton. You do not want to go to jail, Peyton.* I tell myself. This dude is so lucky we're not back on the block. I'd have my brother deal with him real quick, stank breath and all. "Sir. Yes, sir."1…2…3…4…5…breath 6…7, counting to ten again to calm myself down. I can do this. It's only four years, I tell myself. Oh shit, I mumbled a little too loud.

"What did you say, little girl?"

"Nothing, sir." He's standing so close to me, his lips are touch mine. Looks me square in the face.

"That's what I thought. You think you bad because you're from Compton. Your ass will stay up all night until you pee in that cup. Do you hear me?"

Dripping with anger, I respond, "Sir. Yes, Sir. "*I probably won't be using the bathing suit that I packed*, I think to myself. After the fourth week of boot camp, I started to feel better about the military. I stopped getting cursed out by my company commander, I started to learn my job, build relationships and dare I say, I started to like the Navy.

Four years went by quickly. One war, a series of bad and good relationships, world travels, and that promise that I made to myself was still there. Today is the day. May 23, 1992. Deep inside I know that it was the war that put the nail in the coffin for me. That and the racism, favoritism, low paying salary and the bad food. I survived one war, Desert Storm, and was clear that I would never be a part of another war.

Getting out of the military was quickly approaching. I spent a lot of time preparing for life outside of the military. Prior to getting out of the military, I got another "snippet" of what life had in mind for me. To be honest, I cringed at the thought of going back to LA. I want to go back but wasn't sure what I was going back to. Even though I had a tumultuous relationship with the military, I excelled; growing in rank and responsibility every year.

After my initial two year struggle to get settled and find my way; several disciplinary actions, meetings with the captain later, I had finally succumbed to being a soldier, and I was excellent at it. I stopped refusing to salute officers, being rebellious and cursing out my platoon leaders. I started to take initiative and embraced leadership. I'm not sure when it happened, but I grew up. My change in attitude didn't go unnoticed. The base commander looked out for me and even encouraged me to become an officer. He said I was a natural born leader and influencer. He said, he liked the passion that I had and the way that I stood my ground when necessary. "Those attributed, people followed" he said. I listened intently, but I knew. I knew, because of the continued life orchestrated blessings that gently and sometimes painfully reminded me that I was destined for greatness and that I had little choice in the matter.

It was bittersweet, but it was time for me to be great as a civilian. But where? How? I was looking for specifics but wasn't getting a clear direction. I wandered around aimlessly for a while. I became frustrated and started to resent God for abandoning me yet again. I hated when he played the disappearing act game. I hated this feeling of leaving of him leaving me hanging, when he doesn't give me the full story, just half of it, and then he disappears. Snippets. A sick joke.

I spent my early days out of the military trying to find direction and asking, no begging, for another snippet - something that made sense this time. He'd never disappeared this long before. So far, I've been working as a security guard, trying to find a job and asking the same question every hour…for months…"God, where are you?" Uh, hello?! God, where are you?" Did you forget God, "I'm out of the military now. I'm back home in LA, and frankly it's not funny anymore." WHERE ARE YOU? Hello? God? You know you got me living with my momma and she's getting on my nerves. Too many damn people in this house, people drinking and eating up your stuff.

The period of waiting on God was rough. I felt like a loser most days. I just kept trying - anything and everything. I signed up for the police academy. Yes, the LAPD Police Academy. I figured the LAPD ain't so bad. At least I'd have a gun. I was excelling at pre-police academy until one day I did a ride along and the cops brought me home. I went from sitting in the back of the police car smiling to an instant look for bewilderment and fear when Officer Thomlin turned onto my street. The look I got from the neighborhood gangsters as I was getting out of the police car was all I needed to see. I knew that needed to re-think my decision to join the academy immediately. I also tried my hand at being a fire fighter. I think I lost about ten pounds my first day of training, so that career choice ended quickly. Plus, I hated being hot, and I did not want my pretty face to burn up. That would ruin my open casket funeral service.

I was starting to feel desperate. I was going to school and working full time. I wasn't making a lot of money and was struggling to pay my rent. Once I was so desperate, I was going to try my hand at stripping. Yes, stripping. I wasn't even sure that I would be good at it but I figured I didn't really have to be, as long as I could move my hips and look sexy, which came easy for me, I'd be good. I got out of class and decided today was the day that I was going to get some balls and go. I got into my car, changed into my three inch heels, and nervously drove to the club. One last look in the mirror to make sure my makeup looked worthy of a stripper and a deep long sigh. "I'll only do this one time", I tell myself, all the while thinking, God where are you "I'm starting to do dumb shit now, in case you didn't notice." I smirk at myself, thinking I just cursed at God. I walk into the club. Its dark-- really dark except for a light near the stage where I see two men talking. An older gentlemen and a younger gentlemen who looks sort of familiar. They both look at me and I begin to walk toward them. I catch myself mid walk and switch up my walk to a slowed down sexier version. As I get closer, I stop dead in my tracks. The owner is facing me the younger guy is positioned just so that I could see the side of his face, yet his back was facing me. That guy looks so familiar. He continues to talk to the club owner and now I'm think, his voice sounds so distinct and famil…oh shit! That's the guy from my algebra class. Before I could even finish my sentence, I leave. It was not a causal walk out of the club either. It was more like The Road Runner meets Flo Jo. It was a loud and abrupt departure. I'm sure the club owner and my classmate thought I was a crack head.

On my way home, I silently vowed that I would never think that low of myself again. I didn't look in the mirror though. I would've burst into tears if I had. Instead, I just make a solid and non-negotiable truce with myself.

I continued on at the community college for a good while before God decided to make an appearance. Working and going to school is how I spent most days for a few years. Pleading with God to explain to me that, if the plan was for me to be great, why come I wasn't? I really wanted to know, and I wanted this get a glimpse of your God given greatness- small snippet- BS to be over. I was done! Frustrated and exhausted!

I've been attending this community college long enough to be finished by now, but my work schedule interferes with my school schedule, I keep having to drop classes only to pick them up the next semester to only drop them again. The feeling of being trapped is now beginning to feel like quick sand. Stuck. No way out. I'm looking around for help from my family, friends, anyone at this point. They're trapped too, except they don't know it.

\*\*\*

The thing about God is, he never shows up in the way that you expect him to. In October, 1997, I was planning to visit my friends in Washington, DC. They attended Howard University and it was homecoming time. From what I had heard, Howard homecoming was the place to be. Puffy, and other celebrities would be in full effect. If I played my cards right, I'd find me an educated male student who'd willingly sweep me off my feet. I was really looking forward to the trip until I got laid off one week before the trip. Same shit, different day. If I had ten cents for all of the times that I had a job and got laid off, fired, or downsized, I wouldn't have to work because I'd be filthy rich. Nevertheless, I needed the break and I would get a chance to see my friends from high school who were alums of Howard. I was secretly jealous of them. I longed to have a degree, to be educated, to be a part of the talent tenth. They were fortunate enough to have parents with degrees. They were contributing to society and could proudly say that they were college graduates.

I, on the other hand, was still trying to figure it out. If I could just go to college, the doors would be open for me. I thought about it daily. I had managed to complete five classes over the course of a few years at the local community college. I figured I'd get there some day. Graduating from college at 50 wouldn't be so bad. I'd seen a lady graduate at age 65 last summer at my good friend, Angela's, graduation. I was so impressed and motivated seeing her scoot across the stage in her scooter. I also remember asking the Lord to be kind enough to allow me not to graduate from college and die in the same week.

Stepping off the plane, I immediately knew that I was on the other side of earth. I-T W-A-S C-O-L-D. Like COLD. I didn't even want to greet Chrissy and Kia until we got inside. It had been far too long since we saw each other. We hugged and giggled as though we were still in high school. On our way to the game, we caught up on life's happenings, successes, relationships and the people who had made complete asses of themselves since high school. I didn't mention the fact that I had been laid off and how much of an ass I'd felt like over the course of the last few years. It was all about those other low lives, not me.

Stepping on Howard's campus was like stepping inside a landmine. The campus was electric. I felt smart immediately. People were everywhere. It was peaceful and crunk at the same time. I was in the midst of the talented tenth, live and in color. I was trying to contain my excitement but the smile on my face was like a permanent marker. The football game was just as electric. Alumni were celebrities, fraternity boys and sorority sisters representing with their colors, dancing, stepping and re-connecting with their friends. The band was like no other band that I'd ever seen. Majestic with so much swag. I saw a lot of cute guys too. *I could get use to this collegiate atmosphere*, I thought to myself. And then, half time happened. Oh My Goodness! The crowd was moving to the sounds of the band, the ooh La La Dancers were shaking their tails like they were getting paid. They were about to finish the half time presentation but not before playing the National Black Anthem. Looking around at the people with their fists up, singing, I couldn't help but think about the struggle of black people, how the students of this great university were here because someone paved the way for them. In that moment, I knew that God was talking to me and he was saying "It is time for you to be great."

I mumbled, "I'm moving here," at first in my head and then out loud, "I'm moving here!" It was crystal clear that God was talking to me. I was listening because I liked the sound of his voice. I couldn't wait to tell my mother that I was going to be an alumna of Howard University.

***

I only had a few days left before it was time for me to head home, so I paid a visit to the Admissions Office with hopes of getting information on applying, important dates and a timeline. I had completed a few college level courses at the community college but I wasn't sure if I could get into a university. It's one thing to make a decision to do something; being able to do so was a different story. The admissions office was in the basement of the "A" building.

I walked in and told the student receptionist that I wanted to get information on admission. She asked me to have a seat and she would get an admissions counselor to speak to me. Mr. Jerome Hunt, a thin short man with a thick moustache and coke bottle type glasses clearly had a vision problem with those thick glasses but was nice enough. He asked me my age. I told him that I was 29 and that I'd served in the military and had some college and that I was visiting for homecoming but wanted to become a student. I told him that getting my degree was on the top of my list since getting out of the military, I hadn't been able to focus on school the way I wanted to because I had to work full time. When things got hectic, I had to drop my classes and pick up an extra shift, so I never really had the opportunity to take all of the classes that I wanted to.

He asked me how many credits I had. I told him twenty, embarrassed at that fact.

"No worries," he confidently said, "as long as you have a 2.0 and at least fifteen credits, you can be accepted as a transfer student."

My eyes lit up. "Really? I can?"

"Yes," he said, "I guarantee it. Submit your application, while you're here and I can take care of you."

"Wait, I don't have my transcripts with me."

"No problem, he said, "You can request official copies when you get home." He looked at me, smiled, and said in the weirdest tone of voice, "Consider yourself accepted."

The room started spinning and moving in slow motion. "'Consider yourself accepted'? Can I get that in writing?" I asked circumspectly.

"Why, of course you can. Complete the application and I will give you an acceptance letter. Why are you looking at me like that?" he asked with a smirk on his face.

I hunched my shoulders. "This seems too easy. I feel this is too good to be true."

His smile deepened. "Not at all."

I left, told my friends what just happened, and they were excited. Me? I was confused, numb, excited, and believe it was too good to be true.

I completed the application, brought it back to Mr. Hunt the next day before my flight departed back to LA. He wasn't available to talk but I turned my application in and turned around to walk away. The receptionist who helped me the day before called me just as I was turning the door handle. "Ms. Allensworth?"

"Yes," I say skeptically.

"Mr. Hunt left a letter for you. He said you'd be stopping by. Here, wait, let me get it."

I waited. She came around the desk after a few minutes and handed me an envelope. I waited to get outside before I opened it, not sure what the envelope entailed, and not wanting to be embarrassed. I opened the envelope rather quickly. As promised, it was my acceptance letter. I let it sink in. *Five years from today, I will be a part of the talented tenth. A college graduate. Peyton M. Allensworth, BS.* I reluctantly got on the plane back to LA. I knew I'd be back, and I could hardly wait.

***

Entering the cold historic auditorium, I take my seat towards the front. I wanted the speakers to know that I was serious about my education. Only dumb people sit in the back. Smart people sit in the front, I told myself. There were so many students from all over the world. Black people. I nod, smile at those I make eye contact with, wondering whom I will befriend. Maybe I won't. Suddenly I remember that I am much older than the average student. What am I doing? Who am I kidding? I'm too old for school. The doubt begins to kick in.

"Look to the right." *Oh, snap, they started already. I must've blanked out. Too busy thinking about how my old ass doesn't need to be here.* "Look to the left," the university president continues, "One of you will not be here in four years," he says very deliberately.

Uh, what kind of welcome is that? In all honesty, I didn't really give a damn, because Mr. University President was not talking to me. You see, I had given up everything. Okay, well,

I didn't have shit, but I sold my stove for eighty dollars and my futon couch for one hundred dollars. I was fresh off of being laid off of my job. I had to make this work.

"Where will you be five years from today?" the next speaker asked.

I pondered that question for a long time that night after the transfer orientation. It seemed I was always asking and answering that question. Even before I heard the question, I needed an answer.

I swallowed hard, the lump of fear was bubbling in my throat. I was going to be sick. I knew that finishing school was my way out. I'd started and dropped classes at the local community college more times than I cared to remember. There was nothing waiting for me in California. This was my chance, my only chance. I knew with the very fiber of my being that my sitting in the historic Crampton Auditorium was a God-orchestrated phenomenon. Who in the hell got accepted into a high caliber higher educational institution such as Howard University with no transcripts and on the spot? Me. Peyton Peetie Allensworth, the Girl for whom God has a soft spot, the girl who never has it easy but always has it just right. Just in the nick of time. Another snippet. A big ass snippet.

College was a roller-coaster. Highs, lows and lots of in-betweens. I would go on to pursue my passion. Not necessarily the degrees. But proving others wrong, including myself. The degrees were icing on the cake. I completed a double major political science and business degree, graduated at the top of my class, and went directly to graduate school at Cornell University. Ivy League. Who me? Another snippet. I got accepted into an Ivy League school?? My life looked so different, yet the same. All of this simply from making a choice--choosing to open the door of "more" and closing the door of "lack".

### Greatness Achieved

This journey is not necessarily about more money, more vacations or designer clothes. It is about no longer answering the questions that fear conjures up. Why? Why me? Why now? It's also about making the decision to deliberately stop putting question marks, where God puts periods.

It's late, 3 o'clock a.m. I'm adding the final touches to my dissertation, and sipping on this Pinot Grigio got me philosophizing with my own damn self. I wish Lyles were here. He always knows how to make me feel better. At least he listens without interrupting me. He knows I like to argue, talk shit and be right. He lets me, most of the time. More women should put that in their vows: "I promise to let my wife talk shit and be the boss that she is." Then he says, "I do" and they kiss, fuck and open gifts. Sigh, let me get my ass out of this tub, I'm all in my feelings.

Beep, Beep, Beep…ring…ring…ring, I wake up abruptly and in a fog. Sleep in my eyes, yet trying to come to –to figure out what in tarnation is going on. The TV is glaring. I can hear it all the way upstairs. Lyles left the TV on again. I hate when he does that. Reaching for the alarm to turn it off, wondering why Lyles didn't wake me up. Maybe he had to leave early. He didn't mention that he….Noooooooooooooo, it is not 10:00am! I look at the numbers on the clock again, turning the clock sideways this time as if the numbers would change if I held the clock sideways. I jumped out of bed, thinking about my 9 o'clock meeting that I'm missing. Phone rings again, I look at it. Eight missed calls. Dammit! I haul ass to the bathroom to get showered and brush my teeth. I cannot afford to screw this deal up, I say at least six times to no one in particular. This is the deal of the century for me and I cannot afford to mess it up. My phone ring again. I look at the caller ID. Thank God it's my brother; I can briefly talk to him while I brush my teeth. I answer, thinking, he never calls me. "You don't answer your phone anymore?" Well, hello to you too; I can't talk long, I have a meeting that I'm late for and... "Momma is in the hospital" he says clearly over talking me. I stop. Spit out the Toms toothpaste and turn the water off. "Why, I ask? Is she okay?" I'm not sure he says. What do you mean "You're not sure?" She wants to see you, she asked me to call you. "Peyton, hurry please. I hear the panic in his voice, I say ok and hang up before I know in my throat begins to well up.

I land the very next morning in Los Angeles. Thank God for frequent flyer miles. Lyles and I were able to fly for free. Truth be told, the flight could've been a million dollars, we would've still been on it. Momma means that much to me/us. She sacrificed so much for us, her family. It's the least that we could do. I stayed up all night, worrying and praying, but mostly worrying. I must've prayed three million times "Lord, please let Momma be ok." And she was. We arrived at the hospital, went to the room the front desk directed us to, 5A, the Intensive Care Unit. A puzzled look is on my face. "Why is she in ICU?" I ask Lyles. "Don't worry babe." Let's go, he says as he holds the elevator open for me. Before we could step out of the elevator entirely, I can hear momma, talking to her doctor and nurse "I told you, I'm not eating that and I don't care what you say!" I softly knock on the door, and say "hi Momma" squinting, "Peetie, is that you?" Yes, it's me and Lyles Momma. She sits up, against doctor's orders. "Leave me alone, I can do it" I smile, thinking, this woman gets feistier and feistier the older she gets. Lyles and I help prop her up with pillows. "What are you doing here Peetie?" We came to check on you momma." You didn't have to come all the way here. Doctor Williams, she continues, this is my daughter, Peyton and her husband. They live in Washington, DC and they are very successful and rich. I clear my throat and extend my hand, "Hi Dr. Williams, thank you for taking care of my mother. Dr. Williams and his nurses, smile as we exchanged pleasantries. One rolled her eyes. I smiled at her. I knew what that look meant. Momma was wearing her out. We will be in the waiting room, I say again, grabbing Lyles hand.

Fifteen minutes later, Dr. Williams lets us know that it was okay to visit momma. He wasn't sure how long she would be alert, because she received pain medication which also makes her sleepy. We walk in the room as she is flipping channels trying to find a good station to watch. I sit on the bed, lean over to kiss her. She hugs me and begins to cry. I cry too. "I'm so glad you're her Peetie. You're the only person that cares about me. No momma, that not true, I say with as much confidence as I could. "Would you like some water, I ask her? Yes, water with ice. Lyles heads out the door to honor her request, "We stare at each other for a minute. I lay on the bed, holding her hand. We sit in silence, nothing to be said, the love between mother and daughter is speaking loudly and so powerfully. What happened, did you start to feel sick, I ask?

Realizing that I still didn't know what why she was in the hospital. "I felt fine yesterday, but in the afternoon I started to get a headache. By the time, 6 o'clock came, I could barely see. My head was pounding. I asked your brother to take me to the emergency room last night. I'd rather be safe than sorry, I ain't ready to die." "Always Momma, it is better to be safe." You know Peetie, I'm not going to always be here, but I want you to know how much I love you and how important you and your sisters and brother are to me, she strokes my hair and continue. Unfortunately, God does not want me to be here forever. I'm not sure why, I was hoping that I could out do Moses or Noah and them. I laugh, "Momma, that's old." It sure is she says, no thank you, Moses can have that. Life is meant to be lived well. I've lived well, and I've taught you to do the same. You must carry that message with you. You hear me? LIVE WELL, I agree momma, but sometimes I don't know what that means anymore. I work hard, actually all the time. The money and freedom is nice but sometimes, often times, most of the time, I don't have time for myself. "Then you're not living well Peetie. More silence, then I hear her softly drift off to sleep. Just my thoughts and The Jefferson's sitcom playing in the background keeping me awake.

Momma is able to go home two days later. We spend another day with her before its time for us to return home. It's always hard to say goodbye, but I've been prepping myself all morning long. As I was busying myself with things around her house, cooking, cleaning tidying up; I remind myself, I have to come to see her more often.

"Momma, your food for the next three weeks is in the deep freezer and the refrigerator. They are labeled for breakfast, lunch and dinner." I continue giving her instructions until she interrupted me "Peetie, make sure you think about what we talked about." I play dumb, but I know. "What did we talk about?" "She leans in as if she's keeping a secret from Lyles and whispers, "In the hospital room, LW." Okay, now I am confused, I think to myself, what the heck is LW. "LW, Momma?" Yes, LW she yells, startling Lyles, LW, meaning LIVE WELL." Oooh, I say attempting to act as if I forgot. "Don't you mess around with me Peetie." Take care of yourself. "I am Momma, I promise." Lyles chimes in, "How?" "How what?" "How are you going to take care of yourself?" I glare at him. He smiles, "How?" he asks again. I paused to answer the question. I'd drifted off to envision how I was going to kill my husband for a few moments. "Um, I don't know, I have to think about it." Well, that's fair, momma says. I'll tell you what, I nominate myself as your accountability partner for this exercise and I would like for you to go home, unpack, get settled and in one week, I'd like for you to write me a letter detailing how you're going to live well." Huh?" I say. Lyles chimes in again, "Oh that's a great idea momma, I will be sure that she does what you asked her to do." "You're doing it too Lyles" momma says. This time, I laugh, then he laughed and so did momma.

### Live Well

The entire plane ride home, but I kept thinking about my new project pondering, I'll be done with this in no time. I knew what I needed to do to "live well". I just had not time to do it. I would love to take time out for myself, but, I am The Global Vice President of Yerian,

Incorporated which is code for I work 24/7. I can't remember the last time I took a vacation. Lately, I escape by taking warm baths and drinking good wine. Now I'm intrigued, I take out my calendar in search of the last time I took a real vacation. I look at this year's calendar; last year's too, nothing. I asked Lyles, "babe, when was the last time we took vacation?" He laughed, "What's that?" "Are you serious, I ask. "Yes", he says. "We don't go on vacation; you're too busy "working." I sensed some tension, so I try to prove him wrong, "we just came from spending a week in New York, I say. "Yea, well, you spent four of the seven days working." "Did I?" a total rhetorical question, but he happily answered, "Yes you did." I sneered at him, but got the message loud and clear. Momma was on to something. I had not lived well or with intention in a while.

Over the next couple of days, I got quiet, asking the creator key questions; like, how did I get here? I wanted to know where I derailed so that I would never do so again. I numbered my journal from one to five, with the intent of answering the question, what does "Living Well" mean to me today? Because of the successes that I've had in my career, I knew that I had to take action on the things that I discovered or I'd be in the same place next year. So I prepared myself by attaching dates to actionable items. My "Live Well" list looked like:

1. *In order for me to live well, I will take time out for myself daily*. Time with God, myself and my family is none negotiable. Prayer/mediation time: 6a.m., 12noon and 9pm. Family Day: Sundays. Date Night: Thursdays.

2. *In order for me to live well, I will not burn out in order to succeed*. Summer, spring and fall vacation time with no work, laptop or phone and monthly spa appointments, with wine ☺ I must remember to never get so busy making a living that I forget to make a life. Schedule summer vacation within the next 30 days.

3. *In order for me to live well, I must be the best version of me. Every time, unapologetically.* No more apologizing unnecessarily. More laughing. Will practice in the next board meeting.

4. *In order for me to live well, I must remember that I was created for a purpose.* This is tied to No.1. As I get quiet, I will learn what my purpose is in this season of my life. I will read daily devotionals journals to see what God reveals to me.

5. *In order for me to live well, I must give my time and talents to help others.* Mentor college students at my alma mater. Schedule meeting with school to discuss options.

Therefore, what does your Live Well list look like?
Don't have one, I encourage you to create one like I did. You see, you only get one life. ONE. As momma says, *"You get one life to live, but if you live right, once is enough."* Each and every day is a precious gift. Subconsciously, we know this but we don't often manifest the realness of this fact.
If today was your last day on earth, would you be happy with the legacy you are leaving? The work that you've done? The lives that you've impacted? Would you be happy with you?
Think about it!

# About the Authors

## Linda Diaz

**Linda Diaz** has been blessed to be a mother of two daughters and a grandmother to one granddaughter. With her children, they all served as family of volunteers in English bulldog rescue, transport, animal shelters, Earth day events and community improvement.

Linda never liked to share her life's journey and kept so much private, until her life came crashing down on her February 16, 2013, when Linda's 15 year old daughter, Lauryn Santiago completed suicide.

Still in shock and grief, in May 2013, Linda became a volunteer field advocate in Mental Health and Suicide Prevention. Linda takes great pride and honor to be an advocate for our youth and to assist with bringing awareness to Depression, Bullying as well as the Prevention of Suicide.

In hopes to save lives, Linda works hard to share her personal tragedy and loss of her beautiful daughter, to inspire HOPE in our youth and to help them see a brighter tomorrow, for they are NOT alone.

## Linda's Acknowledgments

To my cherished loves LoLa, Andre and Liha, who provide me with the love and strength to make it through each day for a brighter tomorrow.

*"Laugh when you can,*
*apologize, when you should,*
*and let go of what you can't change,*
*at the end of the day, they are still with you."-Lauryn Santiago*

## Norra Prescott

*Receive Mercy and Find Grace* is **Norra Prescott's** writing debut. She is passionate about her commitment to God, marriage, and the institution of forgiveness. She believes that everyone has actions that they will have to reconcile with God. She believes that the beginning of that is asking for forgiveness of those wrongs. This story focuses on seeking mercy for the selfish wrongs that families can inflict on one another.

Norra consults with married men and women to avoid falling prey to the temptations that they may feel. She assists them with finding the root cause of their temptation. She advises them about the the pain that may be inflicted not only to their family, but the inner and outward turmoil infidelity causes themselves. She works closely with women whose battle with infidelity is often overlooked as statistically it occurs more often with husbands than wives. She shares her experiences and lessons from other's experiences to educate about infidelity in a down to earth, non-judgmental manner. Prescott advises those in her ministry to imitate Joseph and flee from sexual enticement.

## Norra's Acknowledgments

Norra would like to thank the lovely contributors of this book, her family, and friends that have supported this effort. I hope you are educated and entertained by this book. I pray that each of you that are touched by our words.

God Bless.

# Wendashia Ray

**Wendashia Ray** is a passionate poet, blogger and author. Inspired by the gift of faith and authors such as Maya Angelou, Chinua Achebe, Nikki Giovani, and Jane Austin; Wendashia artistically puts her pain on paper through autobiographical works, fiction and poetry. As a survivor of teenage dating violence, she is passionate about empowering girls and women. Her experiences of **yesterday** have shaped who she is today; and who she is today is reinventing the Wendashia of tomorrow.

Wendashia's passion for education landed her in Washington, D.C. where she studied International Affairs and Computer Science at the George Washington University. Wendashia's positive energy and motivation comes from God, her husband, her two daughters and her son. She is currently a full time student pursing a degree in Business Administration. Professionally, Wendashia consults on projects, and she is a freelance proposal writer. Wendashia often writes spiritual poetry and affirmations for special events and programs. In addition, she provides original works upon request.

The loss of those who served as part of her lifeline--her father, and both or her grandmothers--left Wendashia anxious and fearful of loss. Through her heart to serve she has transformed that fear into something productive by working with the Comfort Ministry at her church and by using her gift of writing to comfort others who are suffering from their own loss. Wendashia believes in embracing Faith, Family, Friends, Focus, and Follow-Through.

## Wendashia's Acknowledgments

To God, The Creator, The Great I AM. Thank you for the new mercies each day. Thank you for forgiving me and loving me in spite of me. I am truly grateful for your grace and your abundant blessings.

To my earthly king, when I first held your hand I knew you were my "forever." Thank you for loving me, supporting me, and being the man of my dreams. You are the epitome of strength, honor and hard work. Thank you for being the gift from God that you are.

To my heaven on earth--my beautiful children--you are my gifts from God. I love you three with my whole heart. God gave me the most amazing son in the world. Thank you, son, for being the birthday gift sent straight from heaven. To my first born daughter, you inspire me with your wonderful spirit and your amazing talent, you are a dream come true. To my baby girl, through you I have learned to be strong and push the limits, thank you for coming into my life and restoring hope.

To my mother you are elegant, you are determined, you are excellent. You motivate me through your beautiful heart, struggles and triumphs. Thank you for giving me the best so I will continue to strive for the best. Your struggles gave me my strength! I love you!

To my siblings, when you came into my life, I knew I needed to be my best. Thank you for being the gifts that give me motivation. So much love and laughter, there is no other bond like ours and I am truly grateful. I love you and admire you. Claude and Shakara thanks for your helpful advice and consultation.

To my chosen family, "We dropped the In-Law a long time ago." To my mother and sister in love, thank you for all of your love and support. To the coolest father in love in the world and his beautiful wife, I could not have asked for any better. My family-in-love is more than I could have ever dreamed of, and I cannot express how much I love you.

To Grandpa: Thank you for all of the love, support and sacrifice. You are my hero. Keep "taking it all in stride."

To my God-parents thank you for all of your unconditional love and support. Thank you for the amazing examples that you are and for always being there for me.

To Aunt Tammy, thank you for the God in you and the sunshine you bring to my life each and every day. You are a gift from God and I am truly grateful for you. You gave me the love of the library, now I have a book on library shelves around the world.

To my aunties I thank you for your strength, beauty, hard work and unconditional love. Thank you for the countless prayers, love, encouragement and smiles.

To my uncles, thank you for stepping in and being my father figures. You have encouraged me and have given me the strength to persist.

To my saints, Daddy, Grandma and Big Ma; I remember everything you told me but I miss you so much my heart hurts still. You wanted great things for me…I'll stay on the journey I promise as I look to the hills whence cometh my help, my help cometh from the Lord (Psalms 121)

To the Dynamic women of Delta Sigma Theta Sorority, Incorporated, thank you for encouraging me to use my talents to serve, empower and uplift my community. To my line sisters you have had my back no matter what-I love you forever—Relentless.

To my entire family, for all the prayers, love, encouragement, good times and support that is out of this world thank you! To my cousins, I am so grateful for all of the love and never-ending support. You all are all amazing and you inspire me. Family, you are my earthly angels and I pray that God continues to pour his blessings upon our family for generations upon generations.

To my friends who enlighten me and bring me joy. Thank you for always encouraging me and supporting me and accepting me no matter what. To my SWANDIF, my power prayer partner, my closest sister friends, thank you for lots of prayers, laughs, and tears. You bring me so much joy and I love you.

To my co-authors, thank you for the crazy faith to believe we can do the impossible. As we try to change the world, one word at a time, I am grateful for our bond and our trust that we have. Through all the ups and downs, we pressed through. I love you.

## Tamara Stallings

**Tamara Stallings** is the founder and CEO of Go B Great, a career and personal branding firm. She is a sought-after career strategist who combines her more than 20 years of experiences as a human resources leader in global organizations and her experience in the U.S. Navy to form a unique, relevant and refreshing company geared toward individuals who want to maximize their personal power and uniqueness in the changing world of work. She is a frequent guest on numerous career blogs and produced over 40 career networking events annually for her "B Greater" Community. An expert speaker on topics such as entrepreneurship, personal branding and career fulfillment filled with truth, humor and actionable steps to take to change the trajectory of your professional life. Go B Great!!!!

## Tamara's Acknowledgements

Thank you Lord, for the daily demonstration of your greatness through me. I am humbled and honored. To my mother, Kathy, your strength amazes me. Even at 77 years young, you're still a fighter. I'm in awe of you. To my husband, Tasheen, Our marriage is proof that God favors me. Thank you for cheering me on to victory every day. We are truly #tnt #tagteamchamps. To every person that told me no, turned me away or said I was too loud, short, not pretty enough, not skinny enough, too fat, or to insert your negative opinion here- _____ THANK YOU! I'm so glad that I didn't listen to you.

## From The Authors

To God, the Father—through you all things are possible. We give ALL Thanks to you!

To our readers, may you be blessed, educated and empowered by our stories and have the courage to share your stories too!

Fabiola Jean- Louis, your talent made our story visible to the world. We cannot thank you enough for your hard work, dedication and passion for this project. You took our stories and created the artistic canvases that captured what was in our hearts and minds. You were the final blessing that made this a reality. You are a genius and we are grateful that you are part of this team. We love you!

Gael Jean-Louis, your talent is extraordinary. Thank you for all of the advice, patience and for your work in designing the font and logo layout of COVER. Thank you for being a part of the V4 family.

To Linda Cashdan and Bethany Penn, you took us from brainstorm to book. Thank you for all of your editing services, advice and hard work.

To the women of Turning P.A.G.E.S. Book Club-Passionate, Audacious, Gifted, Educated, Successful and so much more, thank you for the meeting that Sunday afternoon when we discovered our stories matter—we matter. Because of you, this book is a reality.

To It Schelle Be Done Event Coordinators (Tishelle and Rachelle), thank you for the valuable advice, patience, event coordination and management. Everything you do is extraordinary and we are truly grateful for all you have done to assist us.

To Queensview Creative Studios, thank you for your amazing marketing and creative assistance.

To JM designs thank you for your awesome web design talent and putting our concept on the web.

To Leyla Lockhart, thank you for your support and for honoring us as the MC of our launch reception and signing.

To the peer review committee Allison, Karen, Loryel, Courtney, Miaya, Latasha and Lakeeshia thank you for your review of our manuscript and your constructive criticism and advice.

To Brianna Schenk and Tonic Restaurant, thank you for giving us a great start with an amazing launch!

To Tasheen Stallings, thank you for your amazing photography expertise, and capturing all of the V4 official events.